W9-BIN-169

Fran Banks

Harlequin Presents..

Other titles by

MARGARET ROME
IN HARLEQUIN PRESENTS

Other titles by

MARGARET ROME
IN HARLEQUIN ROMANCES

Many of these titles are available at your local bookseller or through the Harlequin Reader Service. For a free catalogue listing all available Harlequin Presents titles and Harlequin Romances, send your name and address to:

HARLEQUIN READER SERVICE
M.P.O Box 707
Niagara Falls N.Y. 14302

Canadian address:
Stratford Ontario Canada N5A 6W4
or use order coupon at back of books.

MARGARET ROME

cove of promises

Harlequin Books

TORONTO • LONDON • NEW YORK • AMSTERDAM • SYDNEY • WINNIPEG

Harlequin Presents edition published February 1976
SBN 373-70628-6

Original hard cover edition published in 1975
by Mills & Boon Limited

Copyright © 1975 Margaret Rome. All rights reserved.
Except for use in any review, the reproduction or utilization of
this work in whole or in part in any form by any electronic,
mechanical or other means, now known or hereafter invented,
including xerography, photocopying and recording, or in any
information storage or retrieval system, is forbidden
without the permission of the publisher.

All the characters in this book have no existence outside the
imagination of the Author, and have no relation whatsoever to
anyone bearing the same name or names. They are not even
distantly inspired by any individual known or unknown to the
Author, and all the incidents are pure invention.

The Harlequin trade mark, consisting of the word HARLEQUIN
and the portrayal of a Harlequin, is registered in the United States
Patent Office and in the Canada Trade Marks Office.

Printed in Canada.

CHAPTER ONE

ELISE craned forward, her *gamin* face alive with anticipation, as the plane circled and prepared to land. Below in the Caribbean sea, like a great green turtle basking in the shallows, lay Jamaica. At last her enforced exile was over, she was home, and not even Grand'mère's quelling looks or piercing eyes would force her into leaving it ever again!

As the plane dipped she leant back with a sigh of contentment and closed her eyes, needing no visual reminder of the exotic paradise she was about to re-enter. Coastal plain tilting sharply upwards; highways of asphalt and red earth linking villages and townships known to her intimately; steep mountains capped with green foliage; neat pastures and large checker-board cane fields ... She smiled, then experienced a wave of piercing nostalgia as she recalled days of sun-hot labour spent with Jacques helping to harvest sugar cane grown so tall they had felt like orphans adrift in a forest of towering grass.

Jacques! She swallowed hard, fiercely suppressing tears. Incredibly, ten years had passed since last she had seen her childhood playmate. They had spent their last afternoon together on a favourite strip of beach they had regarded as their own. It was private in as much as it was part of the Montague estate, and as Jacques' grandfather, the Comte de Montague, rarely strayed far from the Grand House there had been very little chance of anyone trespass-

5

ing on their privacy. Boyishly embarrassed, he had kicked hard at a pebble when after days of keeping a stiff upper lip she had broken down and begun to cry.

'Why does the Comte insist upon your going away to school?' she had wept passionately. 'He has always seemed satisfied with the reports he has received from Monsieur Monec!'

For the first time within memory she had been conscious of the six years' disparity in their ages when with the lofty contempt of a fifteen-year-old he had replied, 'Everyone must finish his education in Paris, you know that. In time, your turn will come ...'

'Never!' she had interrupted fiercely. 'No one will ever make me leave here!'

She had flinched when he had turned to vent his own frustrated unhappiness upon her defenceless head. 'Girls are so stupid!' he had railed. 'Because we have played together, shared the same tutor, the same secrets, the same punishments, you think we can remain children for ever? "The time must come," Grandpère says, "when a boy has to be trained for manhood." Well, for me the time has come, and it is now!'

Open-mouthed, she had stared at him. The resolute tone, the determined look, the squaring of boyish shoulders—none of these had ever before been evident in the playmate she had known since infancy, the companion whose happy-go-lucky, irresponsible nature had made negative their six dividing years, rendering them as compatible as twins. There and then she had suffered the first

6

pang of parting, the most painful and lacerating pang of all those that were to follow ...

She was not expecting to be met, so when the plane touched down at Kingston she moved quickly through Customs then lost no time hailing a taxi. 'St Ann's Bay,' she directed the driver with a breathtaking smile before settling down to enjoy the last stage of her journey home. She felt qualms of conscience about hiring the taxi for the long drive north across the island because she had used up all her spare cash during the journey from Paris, but she consoled herself with the thought that when she arrived Grand'mère would pay—predictably with a practical Frenchwoman's grumble about unnecessary extravagance.

Strange, she mused as the taxi sped along the main road upwards towards Mount Diablo, one of the highest points contained within the island's central range, how penny-pinching her grandmother had always been. And yet they had never seemed short of the necessities of life, nor even of some of the luxuries. The house in which they lived was small but comfortably furnished, one of the many confined within the boundaries of the huge Montague estate. Food had always seemed to be plentiful because although Grand'mère had a sparse appetite and she herself as a child had regarded mealtimes as a waste of precious time, there had always been plenty of delicacies in evidence whenever Jacques had shared their meals. Up until she was fifteen her education had cost her grandmother nothing because at the old Comte's insistence, Monsieur Monec, the tutor she had shared with Jacques, had remained to continue with her lessons until it was decided that she, too, should finish her schooling in Paris. New clothes had then had to be bought as up until then she had existed happily in skimpy shorts and disreputable tee-shirts, but Grand'mère had not demurred. Quite unruffled, she had run up what had seemed an enormous account at one of the very best stores in the capital. Vaguely, Elise recalled hearing at some time the mention of a pension sufficiently large to keep them both in comfort during her grandmother's lifetime.

Once over Mount Diablo, the road began to dip and her excitement rose as familiar landscape appeared on the horizon—pasture land full of grazing cattle and somewhere hidden behind great spreading trees the Grand House of the Comte de Montague. She peered out of the window, hoping for a sight of Jacques riding the estate perhaps on his favourite stallion, or speeding through the grounds in the wickedly swift sports car he had sworn one day to own. But no sound disturbed the sultry afternoon calm, so with a keen sense of disappointment she slumped back into her seat as the taxi swept downwards towards a small house built into solid cliff overlooking a bay of crystal-clear water.

She would dearly have loved to surprise her grandmother, but as her fare had yet to be paid she had no option but to ask the driver to wait while she called through the open doorway. 'Grand'-mère! I'm home! Can you fetch your purse, I need money to pay the taxi driver!'

With surprising suddenness an erect old lady

appeared dressed all in black, silver hair piled high in an elaborate coronet upon her regally-held head. *'Tiens!'* she rebuked Elise sharply, 'have I wasted the thousands of francs it cost me to send you to an expensive school? Remember your manners, child, a young lady never yells like a street vendor advertising his wares!'

Elise waited with demurely down-cast lashes and a mouth trembling with humour while her grandmother haggled with the driver over the amount of her fare, then when the disgruntled man had driven off with considerably less than he had demanded she flung her arms around the vexed old lady and hugged and kissed her until finally she melted. 'Oh, Grand'mère, darling Grand'mère, how wonderful it is to be home! I hated Paris, loathed that dreadful school and yearned every minute of those long years to be back here with you! I'll never leave you again, nothing on earth could persuade me to, and even having to spend my vacations with those unspeakable cousins now seems worthwhile if only because I know how much more I'll appreciate the contrasting warmth of home!'

With visible restraint her grandmother pulled away, dabbing at forbidden tears with a wisp of lace. 'Such a tomboy still!' she shook her head, trying hard to appear cross. 'What is to be done with you?'

'Oh, but you know you didn't really want me to change!' Elise grinned, wagging a reproving finger. 'After all, how would you cope with a fine lady under your feet all day? Here, there's no lady's maid to do my bidding and no fine gentlemen around to admire my social graces, so is it not just as well that I've refused to be brainwashed into becoming the sort of useless member of society I despise?' Without waiting for a reply, she ran into the house to fling herself on to a window seat and gaze rapturously out of the window to the sea below. 'Parrot fish,' she murmured reverently as if in prayer, 'see, Grand'mère, how beautifully their blue scales flash in and out of the rocks!'

'I have more urgent things to see to!' the old lady snapped, 'supper, for instance.' Then her eyes softening as they lingered over the slim figure hanging half out of the window, she admitted, 'Your favourite rice and peas should please, seeing how little your tastes have changed.'

Five years of boarding school had, indeed, barely left a mark upon the impish urchin in whom the desire for freedom to roam her beloved island waxed as strongly as ever. For her grandmother's sake, she had endured the boredom of lessons in deportment and social behaviour that had formed a major part of the school curriculum; obediently she had traipsed around art galleries and museums within a crocodile of giggling schoolgirls whose main topic of conversation had centred around boys, courtship and eventual marriage. She had remained so detached from such discussions that not unnaturally some of the girls had begun to show resentment.

'Mademoiselle Elise despises our choice of subject!' Janine Nelson, the spoiled daughter of an American sausage king, had scoffed. 'No doubt her mind is occupied with loftier thoughts.'

'Not at all,' Elise had replied with simple honesty. 'As I already know who my future husband will be further conjecture is unnecessary.'

An awed silence had followed this disclosure. 'I don't believe you!' Janine had finally challenged, eyeing her companion narrowly. 'Prove it by telling us his name.'

'His name is Jacques de Montague,' she had replied immediately, her lack of hesitation giving credence to the statement.

'Grandson of the Comte de Montague?' a second girl had squealed, impressed beyond belief by the knowledge that no one in her right mind would dare claim a betrothal to the grandson of a rich aristocrat without just cause. 'Are you saying that you two are actually engaged?'

Elise had shrugged, impatient of her inquisitors. 'There is an understanding,' she had supplied curtly, an answer accepted without question by the majority of the girls who were French and therefore *au fait* with the practice of arranged marriages. From then onwards she had become the recipient of much respect, but she had remained unmoved by this accolade to her maturity. She was out of place amongst girls she regarded as little more than children, she had always known it, and now they knew it too. And she had told no lies—Jacques had insisted hundreds of times that one day she would become his bride ...

Mathilda bustled into the tiny dining-room carrying a dishful of the salt pork, coconut, peas and rice Elise adored. Barely giving her time to set down the dish, Elise jumped up and with a squeal of delight ran to embrace the old cook-nanny-housemaid whose brown face was split by a large white-toothed smile.

'Welcome home, gal!' she chortled, hurriedly setting the hot dish upon the table, then, indignantly, when in her eagerness Elise jogged her elbow. 'Gal, you want fe come and spill it?'

Elise's laughter rang through the whole house; more than just laughter, it was release, final release from bondage, an echo of the happiness she was feeling because now she knew she was well and truly home. 'Oh, Mattie!' she hugged the ample curves until Mattie's starched apron crackled, 'you darling, now I *know* nothing has changed!'

But later, as she watched her grandmother dish out the meal a faint quiver of foreboding feathered across her happiness. Once-capable hands that over the years had soothed, caressed and sometimes firmly punished seemed almost too frail to cope with the serving spoon, blue transparent veins were knotted beneath skin fine as paper and fingers trembled uncontrollably around the weighted handle. Quickly Elise looked up and was momentarily reassured by her grandmother's tranquil expression until prolonged investigation unearthed further disturbing signs—slightly quivering mouth; a network of lines around tired eyes, loose skin on face and neck denoting recent loss of weight.

She chatted lightly while the meal was in progress, pretending enjoyment of the food she was having to force past the knot of fear paralysing her stomach. '*Dear God*,' she prayed, '*don't let anything happen to Grand'mère!*'

With a great effort of will she remained calm

until Mattie had cleared away and disappeared into the kitchen for the last time. The sun was low on the horizon and day breezes from the sea had given way to a night breeze blowing straight from the mountains, but it was still warm enough for comfort as they shared a seat by an open window looking out to sea.

'Grand'mère,' she began to probe, 'have you been unwell while I was away?'

The old lady stirred, her lowered eyelids lifting. She frowned, then held by Elise's steady young gaze, she sighed and confessed, 'A trifling *maladie*, nothing more.'

Elise reached out to take trembling hands in her warm grasp. 'Why was there no mention of any illness in your letters? I would have come home immediately had I known.'

'You have answered your own question, *enfant*. I had no wish to allow what is merely a consequence of age to interrupt your education.'

'A consequence of age?' Elise prodded, determined to know all.

'Tch, tch ... ! A mild stroke, that is all,' her grandmother clicked impatiently, 'extremely mild. As the good *docteur* said—a warning—no more.'

'A warning ... !' Elise sank back, her merry eyes bleakened. 'Then we must certainly ensure that the warning is heeded!'

As if she had been relieved of a burden, her grandmother's mood mellowed and she fell back upon the past, reliving in a way Elise always found fascinating memories of her youth in days made glorious by retrospect. As a child, unable to equate age,

Elise had visualized her grandmother growing up amongst such heroes of Jamaican legend as Sir Henry Morgan, the filibustering scamp who had swilled wine in the wild haunts of Port Royal in company with other swashbuckling pirates, Spanish, English and French who had made the island their hideout and base. Later, she had realized the folly of such misconception, but the romance and excitement of those earlier times had become indivisible in her mind with her grandmother's youth, creating around it an aura of wild exhilaration. The old lady needed little encouragement once the mood was upon her and when Elise begged: 'Tell me more about the Grand House and Jacques' family, Grand'mère,' she hesitated only fractionally before beginning.

'Jacques' grandmother came to the island as a lovely young bride. From the very beginning of her marriage she loved to entertain, and the Grand House was filled with guests all the year round. She especially loved to ride, so much so that while she was expecting her son she stubbornly refused to listen to reason and carried on with the sport regardless of her own safety and that of the unborn infant.' Elise stirred but did not interrupt; she had heard the story many times before, yet there had never been a time when she had not been an absorbed listener. 'In her final month of pregnancy she had a fall,' her grandmother continued, tight-lipped. 'She died, but by some miracle the child lived.'

'He became Jacques' father,' Elise supplied, 'and didn't he, too, die suddenly shortly after Jacques was born?' Elise intently awaited the reply.

Looking as deeply grieved as if the tragedy had happened only yesterday, her grandmother whispered, 'Yes, and his wife also, in a sailing accident, a trio of tragedies that broke the old Comte's heart . . .' She jerked erect, her old eyes clouded by the revival of painful memories. 'I'm tired, I've talked too long. Please help me to my room.'

Once her grandmother had been settled for the night Elise went in search of Mattie. She needed information and nothing that went on on the island ever escaped the old servant's ears. She found her in the kitchen rocking backwards and forwards in her favourite chair, her head wrapped in a gay bandana, nodding rapturously to the rhythm of music blasting from a portable radio.

'Mattie, do you mind, I want to talk to you,' Elise yelled, indicating the offending radio.

'Sure 'nuff, gal,' Mattie grinned, reaching towards the off switch. 'What it is?'

Smiling her amusement at the traditional reversal of words, Elise questioned, 'It's about Jacques, I'm dying to see him, have you any idea when he'll be returning home?'

'Bless you, pickney, he's bin home this past six months, ever since his grandpa's died!'

'The Comte is dead?' Elise drew a surprised breath.

'The old Comte am—new Comte am Master Jacques.'

But Grand'mère said nothing of this, and she and the Comte were such old friends!'

Mattie stopped rocking, her cheery features col-

15

lapsing into a tearful grimace. 'He was a good man, a *gentleman*, and your grandma owed him plenty. When your ma died, poor sickly chile, he stepped in an' helped when nobody in the whole island cared a damn how a lonely widow woman was gonna manage to rear a howling, cussed-tempered grandchile. He cared 'cos he was in the same boat —him being left to bring up Master Jacques—I guess he felt a kinship with your grandma, both of 'em being French and surrounded wid the English, that is.'

Elise left Mattie to her music and wandered outside in the direction of the beach, her mind occupied with her grandmother's puzzling silence on the subject of the old Comte's death. The old lady had always been reluctant to impose upon the relationship existing between the two families, impressing always upon Elise that although a friendship had been allowed to develop between herself and Jacques she must never at any time forget to treat him with the respect due to a member of the *aristocratie*.

She chuckled aloud, remembering many acts of impudence that would have shocked the old lady rigid had she known of them. The times, for instance, when she had pummelled Jacques' bare brown chest with clenched fists in retaliation against his aggravating teasing, and the day she had rained a volley of pebbles upon his grinning face, ceasing only when a particularly sharp piece of flint had drawn blood from a cut on his cheek, leaving a scar he would carry for the rest of his days . . .

She hugged herself in the darkness as happiness

bubbled like a spring within her. Jacques was here on the island waiting as he had so often promised, to make a permanent companion of the girl with whom he had shared so much: 'Once we are of age,' he had stated solemnly, 'I will seek permission from your grand'mère and my grandpère for us to marry. Until then, we must be patient, but meanwhile wear this ring as a token of my promise.' Her hand lifted to the fine gold chain which for ten long years had held hidden the secret they had dared not share with an adult world. Tenderly she withdrew the ring, touching reverently in turn each tiny stone—a ruby, an emerald, a garnet, amethyst, a second ruby and finally a diamond, remembering the delight they had felt upon discovering that the initial letter of each stone spelled out R-E-G-A-R-D.

'Thank you, Jacques,' she had accepted with all the sincerity of a nine-year-old who had yet to experience more than a friendly hug or brotherly pat from her young suitor. 'I adore my regard ring, I'll wear it always.'

Smiling at the memory, she turned to retrace her steps back to the cottage. Tomorrow she would go in search of him but, the island grapevine being what it was, there would probably be no need. News of her arrival should bring him hot-foot to her door.

CHAPTER TWO

EARLY next morning Mattie shook Elise awake. Startled, she jerked upright, her eyes questioning the worry etched upon the old servant's face. 'Madame won' waken, 'ave bin tryin' this ten minutes past, but she just won' answer. You come try, Missus Elise, a's right worrit!'

On terror-winged feet, Elise sped to her grandmother's room, yelling instructions to Mattie to call a doctor as she ran. The figure in the bed seemed ominously still. Checking her speed, Elise tiptoed nearer. 'Grand'mère,' she pleaded with soft urgency. 'Can you hear me, please give some sign if you can …?' But sparsely fringed eyelids did not lift from waxen cheeks and no murmur came from still lips. Elise sank to her knees at the side of the bed, too numbed to think, shocked by the knowledge that her spirited, omnipotent grandmother was in reality no more than an ailing and frail old lady. For seeming hours she sat caressing icy, blue-veined hands, but in fact less than fifteen minutes had passed by the time Mattie arrived accompanied by a doctor who, after one sharp glance at Elise's stricken face, ordered her out of the room.

'Give her tea with plenty of sugar,' he directed Mattie, 'and keep her downstairs until I've time to attend to her!' He was the sort of man one did not argue with, young, energetic, possessed of a jutting, self-willed chin, so Elise obeyed.

She was in the kitchen, perched tensely on the

edge of a chair, when he walked in and nodded towards the teapot. 'Can you spare me a cup?'

'We sure enough can!' Mattie rose with alacrity, but he shook his head and directed,

'You go upstairs to Madame Calvet, she'll need you when she awakes.'

Elise raised dulled eyes. 'You mean she isn't dead?' The whispered question rose hysterically high.

'Whatever gave you that idea?' He poured himself some tea. 'Madame Calvet has mistakenly taken two of the sleeping tablets I prescribed instead of one, as directed. She'll suffer no after-effects other than a slight dizziness and perhaps a headache when she awakes, but I would feel much happier if some responsible person were to dole out her pills in future. Old people are very apt to swallow pills, then, forgetting they have taken them, later take more. Who are you?' he shot out, 'a visitor, or a neighbour, perhaps?'

Even the relief she felt at his words could not drown the resentment his curt manner had aroused. A typically self-assured Englishman, she fumed. 'I'm Elise Portland. Madame Calvet is my grandmother and I live here.'

He did not seem impressed. 'Then might I advise that in future you spend more time at home? Your grandmother will not admit to it, but lately she has not been well. She needs rest, freedom from strain, and above all,' his eyebrows beetled as he set down his cup, 'no shocks of any kind. It's her heart,' he explained, softening at the sight of her trembling mouth, 'I'm sorry, but it's best that you should be prepared.' With these words, the doctor departed.

Long after he had gone Elise remained staring blankly at the wall, trying to come to terms with a situation she had suspected the previous evening but which was now a concrete fact. Grand'mère, her beloved and only relative, was very ill. If she should die what a gap she would leave! Who would she turn to for love and comfort once Grand'mère had gone? She had never known her mother, Grand'mère's only child who, according to Mattie, had died supposedly of complications arising from childbirth but in reality because the no-good Englishman she had married had deserted her before the birth of their child. Being an orphan had not bothered her as a child, indeed, it had seemed just another of the many things she and Jacques had in common. 'Jacques!' She breathed his name, comforted by the reminder that as long as she had him she would never be alone.

By midday her grandmother was wide awake and anxious to be up. Annoyed with herself for precipitating a crisis, she snapped off Elise's head when she suggested she should take things easy for the rest of the day, contrarily demanding that her granddaughter should accompany her on a walk to the nearby shops.

'But there's no need, I can get everything you want, and the sun is so hot . . . !' Elise protested.

'Nonsense!' Madame snapped, 'I insist we go together!'

The shops were clustered around a sleepy harbour where fishing boats idled on a slight swell, their holds empty, decks swilled clean, ready and prepared for the next harvesting of the sea. On a nearby strip of beach, shrubs, almond trees and sea-grape flourished profusely around coconut trees with roots thrust vigorously into good earthy soil. In the first shop they came to, Elise settled her grandmother into a chair hastily supplied by the proprietor, then wandered outside, knowing she would not be missed for at least half an hour. All Jamaicans love to bargain and to her grandmother shopping was not merely the putting down of money and the taking away of goods, but an opportunity to haggle and a pleasant way of engaging in conversation.

Perched on a rail adjacent to steps leading down to a wooden jetty, she looked out to sea, following the progress of a speed boat making towards shore with sparkling spray churning in its wake. The two occupants seemed to be enjoying themselves immensely, a girl's screams and a man's laughter rose above the noise of the powerful motor. Elise watched as it slowed down, then glided to a stop alongside the jetty, envying the long-legged elegance of the blonde beauty being helped ashore so chivalrously by the daredevil whose handling of the boat had betrayed a flamboyance akin to recklessness. The girl seemed blissfully contented in his company, however, and although she knew she was being rude, Elise continued to stare at them as laughingly they progressed towards the end of the jetty. It was not until they were near enough to be recognized that something dormant inside her began to stir. A cry was strangled in her throat as she scoured the dark, piratical features, the long, lithe frame, the dancing eyes—shockingly blue in a face tanned dark as a deep sea mariner's. Her suspicion was confirmed when the girl called out: 'Jacques!' in pretended terror when her foot slid across slippery boards, and a great tide of feeling swamped Elise, rendering her tongue still, her limbs immobile and her breath suspended for long, painful seconds.

Without a glance they made to pass her, his sleeve almost brushing the arm of the urchin sprawled inelegantly across the harbour rail, then when his sharp ears caught the sound of a constricted choking he swung round alarmed to peer down at her. 'What's wrong, *mon enfant*, are you ill?' When mutely her eyes raked his beloved features he instructed his companion, 'Quickly, Camilla, enquire whether anyone in the nearby shops knows this child, we must try to find her mother!'

Scarlet-faced, Elise jumped down from the rail. *Enfant! Child!* he had called her—*twice!*

'Jacques, don't you know me?' she stammered, confirming his impression of childhood. 'It's Elise!' she urged. 'Elise Portland!'

Amazement replaced the indolent concern he had been prepared to expend upon a seemingly ailing child, then, as his bright blue gaze explored a small brown face with tip-tilted nose, engaging, over-generous mouth and brown eyes adoring as a puppy's, recognition flared. *Elise? Ma Petite amie? C'est impossible!* A grin of pleasure flashed white against tanned cheeks as swiftly he pounced to lift her, feather-light, into arms that twirled her in a breathtaking circle high above his head.

'Put me down!' she stormed, humiliatingly aware of the amused stare of his companion. This was not the way she had envisaged their meeting! His attitude was all wrong, he ought to have recognized immediately that she was now quite grown up and mature enough to be accorded the same courtesy he had so ably demonstrated towards his girl companion, who was now openly laughing.

Furiously, she kicked and wriggled until he was forced to set her down. If nothing else, the amber-flashing storm signals in her eyes seemed to prod his memory alive. 'Still the same little firebrand,' he reacted tightly, rubbing a throbbing shin. 'Madame Calvet must be less than delighted with the achievements of the exclusive school which, if my memory serves me correctly, purported to transform even the most flagrant of tomboys into a presentable young lady.'

'Oh, Jacques, be fair!' trilled the smiling vision by his side. 'Some of the blame must rest with you. Confess now, would you ever dream of greeting *me* in such a rough, undignified way?'

As Elise and he eyed one another like adversaries, each as angry as the other, the rebuke, though mild, became immediately effective.

'*Touché!*' He relaxed, soothed by the girl's coaxing smile.

He reacts like a cat that's just been stroked! Elise thought, fiercely resentful of the other girl's possessive assurance. He never used to be so malleable, so *pliant*!

She was consequently aloof when he tendered an apology. 'Mademoiselle Elise,' he swept a mocking bow, 'forgive me, my manner of greeting was *diabolique*, I must earnestly beg your pardon.'

Aware that they both were expecting a rude, gauche reply, she inclined her head and countered with dignity, 'Your apology is accepted, *monsieur*. Every man at some time in his life is allowed one small lapse.'

Swiftly his head jerked up and she suffered a prolonged, blue-stiletto stare. Then to her surprise colour the shade of shame darkened his cheeks as quietly he offered, 'Thank you, perhaps now you will allow us to escort you home?'

The girl with the face of an angel and the deportment of a queen did not react favourably to this suggestion; immediately her lips pouted and the glance she directed towards Elise was full of annoyance.

'But how remiss of me!' he exclaimed. 'You two have not yet been introduced. Camilla, may I present Elise Portland, a very old friend, though considering her extreme youth you must find that hard to believe—we played together as children. Elise—Camilla Nelson, a friend of not such long standing but a very dear one nevertheless.'

Elise wondered if the sudden plunging of her heart had left any visible sign on her too expressive face. The way he was smiling down at Camilla, the tenderness with which he had spoken her name, his eagerness to exploit any opportunity to reach out for her, to touch her hand, to smooth a flying wisp of hair from her eyes, to steady with a firm grip around the waist—his every action was the action of a man deeply infatuated!

She could barely manage a nod of acknowledgement towards the girl she knew instinctively was all wrong for him.

'A childhood friend, you say?' Camilla commented, shrewdly noting the mature arc of breasts beneath a baggy tee-shirt and the shapely curve of hip and thigh disguised by shapeless jeans but obvious to eyes that wished to see. Then in the manner of a general planning a campaign she decided upon tactics. 'It does seem incredible that one so young could have shared your childhood. You must, even then, dear Jacques, have projected the same fascination for the immature as you do today.'

He grimaced. 'If you are referring to your young sister and her awesome school friends then all I can say is I am more than grateful that a window separated us the day we paid her a visit. *Quelle horreur!*' he shuddered. 'I felt in danger of being torn limb from limb!'

Camilla's laughter was an extension of her personality, Elise judged, attractively monitored so as never to be in danger of losing control. 'Jacques was with me when I dropped off a parcel at my sister's school,' she explained to Elise. 'We were just about to leave when a horde of giggling girls who suddenly appeared at a classroom window seemed to go berserk at the sight of him. The poor dear went quite pale!'

'I was terrified,' Jacques assured her with a grin. 'In future, the Rue de Matin will be strictly out of bounds whenever I am in Paris.'

Elise's polite smile became suddenly fixed as the inconsequential conversation became fraught with

25

danger. The Rue de Matin was where her old school was housed and an explanation of why some of Camilla's modes of expression were tantalizingly familiar was suddenly apparent. *Camilla* Nelson— *Janine* Nelson! Surely fate had not been cruel enough to deposit a relative of one of her school friends on the island!

Through a throat so dry she sounded barely articulate, she stammered her excuses. 'Please forgive me, I must go, Grand'mère will be waiting. So nice to have met you,' she babbled on, desperate to flee yet honour bound to mind her manners, 'perhaps we'll meet again another day.'

'Perhaps nothing!' Jacques took up. 'Of course we must meet.' Then to her retreating back he called out: 'Tell Madame I will visit her soon— perhaps tomorrow!'

Just as she was nearing the shops Elise saw her grandmother being helped into a car by a neighbour who had obviously offered to drive her home. Thankfully, she shrank back into the shade of a nearby building until the car drove off, then with an ache like iron in her breast she began to run, heedless of the heat, her hair a streaming mane behind her, until she reached the haven she was making for, the cove she and Jacques had made their own.

The cove of promises was deserted, so she threw herself down upon the white sand, fighting tears that might have interfered with the process of thought—such bewildered, confused, unhappy thought! He had looked at her first with the eyes of a stranger—whereas she had known immediately

26

she was in his presence. Even after recognition he had continued to call her *child, enfant.* Then had come the supreme indignity of being tossed in his arms—the arms of an indulgent uncle—when with every fibre of her being she had wanted to press her mouth against his, to feel his lips move under hers, to experience a culmination of the passion that had grown as she had grown, nurtured by promises, fed upon dreams, but far outstripping in maturity the untouched, innocent body within which it was contained.

She screwed tight fists deep into the sand as pain washed over her, wondering why, when shame, humiliation and despair were so lethal, they did not kill. A change of heart on his part she could have understood; excuses to delay in order to bridge the gap left by long separation might have been borne with fortitude if not with grace, but blank disinterest—worse, *avuncular concern,* were emotions she had not expected from him.

Hours later she trailed back to the house, her dispirited movements indicative of the anguish still activating her mind. Mattie's enthusiastic welcome: 'Black crab for supper, honey!' faltered into puzzled silence when Elise passed her without a word. But she was not to escape so easily from her grandmother, who halted her progress upstairs with the firm command, 'Elise, come into the sitting-room, I wish to speak with you.'

'Can't it wait, Grand'mère?' she appealed, inclining her head so that a curtain of hair swept down cheeks grimed with sand and tears.

'No,' her grandmother gently insisted, 'I feel I

may already have waited too long to talk to you.'

Elise followed her into the room and dropped into an armchair, avoiding her grandmother's penetrating look by studying carefully a worn patch on the carpet.

'You have spoken with Jacques?' Madame asked, keenly troubled.

Obviously a denial was unnecessary. 'Why didn't you tell me the old Comte had died?' Elise countered, venting some of her misery into the accusation.

'I waited, hoping that the ties that bound you to the Montague family in the past might have lessened during the years of separation. I see now that it was a vain hope.'

'You wanted me to *forget* the old Comte and his many acts of kindness?' she questioned incredulously. 'To forget Jacques?'

Her grandmother leant forward. 'You *must*,' she insisted, her wise eyes brimming with sympathy. 'Jacques—Monsieur le Comte,' she corrected hastily, 'is in a world apart from you now. The childhood companion is gone for ever, you must accept that, Elise, come to terms with the fact that he is now the head of a very old, aristocratic house and that you as the grandchild of a penniless old woman can lay no further claim upon a family that already has done more than enough to justify our everlasting gratitude!'

'The old Comte must have approved of the close alliance between ourselves and his grandson, why else would he have continued to be so generous and so kind?' Elise submitted quietly.

'Why?' Her grandmother considered thoughtfully. 'Out of pity, I suspect. Jacques' grandfather was a man of high principles, deeply conscious of the needs of others and of his duty towards his tenants. But the present Comte is not of the same mould as his grandfather,' she stressed quickly. 'His love of fast cars, fast horses—of anything allied to danger—is well known to the islanders, and as for his exploits with women ...!' Delicately she dabbed her top lip with a scrap of lace, giving herself time to rally before continuing. 'Even if he were not the Comte de Montague, I would not wish your acquaintance with Jacques to continue. He is wild, that one, as self-willed and reckless as was his mother and, I have no doubt, as cruelly demanding of those who love him!'

Elise rounded upon her then, all her pent-up feelings spilling into her defensive words. 'Jacques is first and foremost a *man*, a glorious animal, so thoroughly human that even his weaknesses can be irresistible!'

Only then did her grandmother betray anger. 'Foolish child!' she rapped, controlling her breathing with difficulty. 'You think yourself in love, but it is merely a childish dream you cherish! As you say, Jacques is a man, a man with an unlimited capacity for gallantry coupled with a rake's desire to indulge it on every occasion! He represents heartache, misery, tears of neglect and nights of jealousy-ridden loneliness! I demand that you put him out of your mind, in spite of his many faults he is still Monsieur le Comte and you, *mademoiselle*, must remember to *keep your place*!'

CHAPTER THREE

ELISE and her grandmother were in the garden gathering flowers for the house when a few days later Jacques made his promised visit. He was alone, as Elise quickly verified with a glance across his shoulder. He had crept up unannounced, startling them both with a pleasantly voiced greeting that distracted their attention from the rose bushes.

'Break not the rose, its fragrance and beauty are surely sufficient,' he rebuked gravely.

'Jacques!' Elise squealed, her too obvious delight bringing a frown to her grandmother's face. At the sight of it his grin disappeared, leaving him with an endearingly solemn expression. Even though she was perfectly aware that she was being deliberately wooed, the old lady's defences were ineffective against his practised charm.

'You are quite right to frown, Madame Calvet, my neglect of you is unforgivable. Will you smile a welcome if I promise to visit you more often, perhaps as often as I used to in the old days?'

'Any offspring of your grandfather's will always find a welcome in my home,' she replied, a smile taking some of the starch from her words.

With the determination of a man unused to experiencing anything less than idolatry from the opposite sex, he began concentrating all his attention upon bringing back laughter to the old lady's lips and the warm regard, which as a boy he had taken so much for granted, back into her eyes. They sat in deck chairs around a white marble-topped table, sipping from tall glasses the fruit nectar Mattie excelled in brewing, an exotic concoction of juices of the guava, soursop, mango, pawpaw, tamarind and grenadilla.

'Delicious!' Jacques tossed back his head to savour the last drops trickling down his throat. 'Mattie is the greatest treasure on this island—my servants are an idle, shiftless lot, especially the cook, whose food is so appalling I'm driven to eating out whenever possible. Entertaining at home is quite out of the question.'

'Obviously you need a wife,' Madame stated. 'Your grandfather never had need to complain about his staff who were old retainers, but Jamaican servants are notoriously covetous of praise and if, as I suspect, you do not bother to show appreciation then the lack will surely show in the quality of their efforts.'

Elise's heart flipped over when he smiled. 'You are very perceptive, Madame,' he congratulated with a twinkle. 'How did you guess that such a course was already in my mind?'

Unnoticed, the glass slipped from Elise's fingers on to the grass when her grandmother leant forward to ask, 'You are considering marriage, *mon fils*?'

For one so debonair, he looked almost boyish. 'I intend proposing this very night,' he confessed, able for once, within the company of his oldest friends, to relax the role of Comte and revel in the sharing of a secret with the two who represented the nearest thing to family left remaining. 'Elise met her a few days ago,' he barely glanced her way before turning back to Madame. 'Her name is Camilla Nelson—a charming creature, don't you agree, Elise?'

Suddenly his attention was upon her, noting signs of distress in stricken eyes and a mouth quivering as if from a recent thrashing. 'I ... I ...' Words of polite agreement would not come and his expression of puzzlement was so hard to bear that after an incoherent mumble Elise jumped to her feet and ran.

There was no rest for her that night, nor during the following days as she waited for the formal announcement of the engagement between Jacques, Comte de Montague and Camilla, eldest daughter and heiress to the fortune of Bertram Nelson, American millionaire. Camilla and her father were staying in the capital's most noted hotel, but even though the width of the island separated them Elise knew that within hours Mattie would receive any noteworthy news via the islanders' grapevine. Each morning she tensed when Mattie made her noisy entrance into the dining-room, and each evening at supper she waited fearfully for words that would shred her heart to pieces. But for some reason confirmation did not come.

Alarmed by her lack of appetite and by the lethargic movements of young limbs once so vitally energetic, her grandmother was forced to remonstrate. 'Child, I know how hurt you must be feeling, but believe me, starving yourself will not change

Jacques' feelings! He must be deeply in love with this girl, and I need hardly remind you that such affection does not easily erase.'

Wearily Elise pressed a hand to her aching head. 'There's nothing you can teach me, no agony I haven't already learned about love, Grand'mère!'

Madame whitened, then after minutes of deep thought came to a decision. 'There is something you should know about Jacques.' When her granddaughter's bent head did not lift she forced herself to continue. 'Just after he came of age, while he was still in Paris, there was a scandal, hushed up, of course, an *affaire de coeur* that did not work out—the silly girl committed suicide.'

She waited, expecting reactions of shock, dismay, even disgust, but instead was astounded when Elise raised her head, disclosing the face of a child but with eyes mirroring the wisdom of a woman. 'I don't care about the scandal, Grand'mère,' she insisted gently, 'nothing you say will change my feelings for Jacques.'

Jeremy Sherlock, Madame's doctor, had formed the habit of visiting her almost every other day, and it was he who informed them that Camilla had left the island. 'She and her father were invited to join a cruise aboard a private yacht that dropped anchor in Montego Bay one day last week, supposedly just long enough to take on fresh supplies. The owner turned out to be a business acquaintance of Mr. Nelson's and he delayed long enough to persuade Camilla and her father to join his party—a not too difficult task, I imagine.'

He shrugged off Elise's resentful stare, more

concerned with the finding of Madame's thready pulse than with parrying the moods of her capricious granddaughter.

'What about Jacques?' she questioned sharply, forgetting in her anxiety that the doctor was probably ignorant of any connection between the Comte and Camilla.

His eyebrows rose. 'I am not a purveyor of gossip, *mademoiselle*,' he snubbed mildly. 'If you want news of that young man I suggest you contact his friends.'

Her grandmother forestalled her irate reply with the gentle apology, 'Please excuse the question, *docteur*, it is not curiosity but concern that prompts Elise to enquire after our very dear friend. His absence is puzzling, especially since only a few days ago he promised to visit us regularly.'

Snapping shut his bag, the doctor advised dryly, 'Save your concern for those more worthy of it, *madame*. The Comte has a surfeit of time and money, together with a host of companions willing to help him spend both. I will call again in a few days.' He rose to his feet, effectively checking any follow-up to the conversation. 'Remember what I said about resting those swollen ankles!'

When he had left Elise and her grandmother stared at each other, wondering at the implication behind his cryptic statement. Clearly, the doctor had no time to spare for Jacques.

'I have a feeling of unease, Grand'mère,' Elise confessed, her brow wrinkling with anxiety.

Madame nodded. 'I, too, am wondering why a girl would leave behind a new fiancé for the sake of a mere sea trip. Could it be . . . ?' She hesitated.

'What . . .?' Elise prompted.

Her grandmother shook her head as if the notion that had presented itself was too preposterous for words, but urged on by Elise's anxiety she continued slowly, 'Could it be that she has turned him down?'

A few nights later, via Mattie, the reason for the doctor's impatience with Jacques was made clear. She burst into the salon where they were relaxing after dinner, her startled black eyes and quivering body communicating suppressed excitement long before her spate of words began. 'Mister Jacques is causin' one heap o' trouble, missus,' she panted. 'A've just this minute heard 'bout his hellraisin' all over the capital this past week or more—drinkin' and larkin' 'bout wid a crowd o' wild uns the divil could've spawned! He's one crazy man, for true! Kingston ain't seen nothin' like his carrying on since Henry Morgan and his buccaneers!'

Elise jumped up. 'How ridiculous, it simply isn't possible!'

Regretfully, her grandmother shook her head. 'It *is* possible and you know it, child. You simply don't want to believe.'

Passionately, Elise spun round to condemn, 'Why are you all so quick to judge him? Simply because he doesn't react to a situation in the way his grandfather did you condemn him as wild and uncontrollable! Can none of you recognize his great need to be loved—completely and wholly loved—for himself and not simply because of his title and his position in the ranks of the wealthy?' She rushed

35

towards the door, hesitating only long enough when she reached it to direct a plea for understanding. 'I love him, Grand'mère! He needs me, so I must go to him!'

Elise discovered that Kingston at night was a hive of pleasure, pandering especially to the tastes of the music-loving Jamaicans, every one born under a dancing star. Orchestras, combos and calypso bands were thumping out tunes, modern in tempo, swinging with rhythm. Laughter spilled through doorways into streets only slightly less crowded than the nightclubs, supper clubs and inns that excited the imagination with such names as The Queen of Hearts, V.I.P. Club, Humming Bird, China Doll, and the Cellar.

She had not stopped to change, and many curious glances were directed towards her slight blue-jeaned figure as quite unselfconsciously she combed the crowded clubs in search of Jacques. As one by one the more fashionable haunts were ticked off her list, she progressed towards a less affluent area where dilapidated buildings with frontages of peeling paintwork and finger-marked glass catered for a more rowdy and less well-dressed clientele. Sailors seemed predominant amongst the customers, and several times she had to dodge the attentions of lonely men intent upon supplying drink in exchange for company. With single-minded determination she pressed on, immune to the dangers threatening a solitary girl let loose in a jungle full of hot-blooded males, standing on tiptoe to see over a mass of heads, listening intently for the sound of a certain voice, craning her neck for the sight of his dark, familiar features, so very dear to her.

It was almost midnight when she found him. Exhausted to the point of collapse, she forced her way through a crowd of brown-skinned revellers gathered in front of a circular stage where native dancers in grass skirts were gyrating to swinging drums, matching the hot rhythm with pounding feet. His companions were by far the rowdiest in the room, their white complexions standing out plainly in a desert of brown. Shrieking girls and young men, more than a little intoxicated, each with the blasé, world-weary look of youngsters possessed of unlimited leisure and wealthy, over-indulgent parents, were urging on the dancers to even greater efforts with whistles and cat-calls piercing enough to override the babble of voices and even the strident cacophony of sound emerging from the band.

Elise pushed her way forward, Jacques' dark head for ever in her sights, until at last she stood panting before him. He and his friends were seated around a table, but in striking contrast to their exuberance he was morose, his chair tipped back, feet planted outrageously in the middle of the table, staring moodily into his glass with a frown so black she felt afraid. He had been hurt, so dreadfully, mortally hurt that all his outgoing love of life had been channelled inward, creating a rapier of self-stabbing hate!

'Jacques ... !' she faltered, ignoring the suddenly attentive stares of his companions. A vacuum of silence fell. All around them people continued to talk and laugh, but as if from afar, the muted sounds an unimportant background to the drama she knew, with dread, was about to begin here.

Not a muscle of his body moved as his glance elevated above the rim of his glass to study the slender figure shivering with apprehension but determined to brave his reaction—whatever the outcome.

One of the girls began to laugh, high-pitched, scornful laughter that was strangled at birth with one look from Jacques' quelling eyes. He swung his long legs to the floor and stood up, kicking away an obstructive chair, then with his eyes fixed upon her defiant face he approached and demanded: 'What the hell are you doing here?'

She blanched, but stood her ground. Nothing would have induced her to betray the terror caused by his resentment and by the hard anger displayed in the face thrust close to her own—so close she could see the small scar she had inflicted so many years ago. Instinct warned her that reproach would be dangerous, in his present mood he was capable of committing any outrage upon any person—ally or not!

Feeling as suspect as a spy amongst brigands, she forced brightness into her smile and turned her answer into a quip. 'I've come to join in the fun!' she flirted, suffering stampeding heartbeats. 'I was bored half to death on the far side of the island, so when I heard about the high jinks you were enjoying in the capital I decided—why not? If Jacques knew how starved I am of fun he would be the first to suggest: "Come and join us"—so here I am,' she finished lamely, wiping sweaty palms down the sides of her jeans.

'Without bothering even to change,' he added sarcastically, his eyes fixed upon the toe peeping out of a hole in her shoe.

'Don't be so stuffy!' she scoffed, taking courage from the reluctant interest his jaded companions were beginning to display. 'I came for a good time and as far as I'm concerned fashion is death to fun! I'm satisfied if my clothes are wearable even if, at times, they may look a little uncivilized. Remember, Jacques,' cleverly she addressed him although her words were aimed at his followers, 'a man can become a creature of his uniform!'

Amusement bubbled within her as gleefully she noted that her barb had found its mark. The imitative pack were each impeccably attired, men in white dinner jackets and black ties and the girls in dresses casually comfortable but correct evening wear, nevertheless. With dawning respect they eyed the impish urchin who, with a few well-chosen words, had indicated that she thought them too conventional and over-dressed—members of a species they themselves purported to despise.

The trap was sprung and they were quick to fall. 'Let's all buy some jeans!' an excited girl yelled, and with a roar of approval the rest agreed.

During their noisy exit Elise felt the stab of Jacques' narrow stare. 'I had forgotten what a cunning little devil you are,' his soft-toned drawl menaced. 'Even as a child you showed a true female's aptitude for getting your own way.'

She countered the remark with an innocent stare. 'My own way?' she queried as he waved her towards a seat at the table.

'I know very well why you are here,' the duel continued. 'You came to save me from myself,' he mocked, 'to rescue me from the perils of self-pity and over-indulgence in the panaceas that mercifully are available to soothe the ego of the rejected male. Camilla has left the island—you know that, of course,' he thrust savagely. 'Probably either she or her father has taken heed of the gossips and the cruise dangled under her nose by a besotted millionaire will give her time to decide whether or not to continue our relationship.'

His pain was her pain; his ravaged emotions were a weight in her breast, his frustration a bitter taste in her mouth. Battening down the sympathy she ached to express, she parried with a casual shrug, 'The role of rejected suitor doesn't suit you, it's completely uncharacteristic. At the moment, because your confidence has taken a whipping, you need a woman—any woman will do. I'm prepared to bet that soon you'll forget Camilla, you might even fall in love—truly in love, I mean, emotionally as well as physically.'

The soupçon of scorn she injected into her words was a masterly touch, it flicked across his raw pride with the touch of hot steel, jerking him erect. The impact when their eyes met was as clashing as swords, but she did not flinch from his displeased arrogance, rather she revelled in the passion directed towards herself—even though its name was rancour.

'As you say, I need a woman,' he clenched. 'And again, *as you say*, any woman will do. So what about you?' he challenged with wicked *diablerie*. 'Do you dare take up once more the role of companion, to soothe me when I am irate, comfort me when I'm distressed and entertain me in my lonely hours as only a woman can?' He leant forward, one scornful eyebrow winging. 'Or are you at heart still too much of an infant to fulfil a man's demands? *Le bon Dieu* knows how much I need a woman's solace,' he laughed without humour, 'but how He and his angels must be laughing at my choice!'

'Flattery,' she projected through clenched teeth, 'was never one of your habits! Very well,' she sparked with anger, 'I'll accept your offer, if an offer it is, I'll undertake to cope with all your demands, but only to prove my point which is that the emotion you feel for Camilla is a mere shadow of the real thing!'

A shutter fell across his eyes, rendering them blank. 'What can you possibly know of love?' he scoffed, raking her boyish outline with an indifference more galling than scorn. Elise winced, but he seemed not to notice, and only then did she realize how far the considerate, fun-loving boy she had loved had been overtaken by the cynical man. Her senses quivered, appalled at the immensity of the task she had undertaken. If he responded to her challenge there would be no quarter expected or given; a future of searing heartache and continuous humiliation hung upon his answer.

He took his time, glancing around the room as if to ensure that no other alternative to boredom was on offer. But all the verve had gone from the entertainment, the dancers had disappeared, even the band had retired somewhere to enjoy a well-earned rest, so, a slave to desperation, he conceded, 'All right, the exercise might not be without its moments of interest. Let's go, Girl Friday, we'll begin by taking this town apart, then squeezing it dry!'

CHAPTER FOUR

Girl Friday: a faithful attendant willing to turn her hand to anything in order to please her master!

The following week was a hectic carousel of manufactured amusement. As restlessly as the pirate ancestors from whose loot and plunder the estate of Montague had reputedly been founded, Jacques pursued every known avenue of pleasure. Water-skiing, riding, skin-diving, tennis, yachting were crammed into every daylight hour, but the physical effort involved in such sports was nothing compared with the sheer stamina needed as each evening was rounded off with a whirling, non-stop tour of the night-spots. He tried Elise to the limit, deliberately adopting a punishing pace in order to force her to admit herself beaten. But she would not allow him the satisfaction of even a small complaint as doggedly she endured the hectic routine, matching his vigour with vitality, his zest with a sparkling exhilaration he did not suspect was a cloak for physical and mental exhaustion.

He bought her clothes—masses of them. Dresses for afternoon and evening wear, smart beach outfits, slim trousers with matching tops, diaphanous lingerie he seemed to take a wicked delight in helping her to choose—simply, she suspected, because his quick eyes noted pink cheeks curiously at odds with the panache she had struggled to display. She had moved away when embarrassment had

43

triumphed, only to be steered back with the cryptic statement: 'Modesty will not keep you warm,' burning her ears.

Her hotel bedroom adjoined his and an outside verandah ran across the width of the two rooms. Breakfast for two was served to her each morning and he joined her simply by swinging his long legs over the verandah rail. On the ninth morning of their marathon pleasure hunt he appeared, fresh as ever, and sniffed appreciatively the aroma of coffee and newly baked rolls. 'Papaya with a sprinkling of lime juice,' he requested when she proffered a choice of fruit. 'Oatmeal porridge does not go with sunshine.'

Hardly daring to meet his satirical glance, she served him, wishing she could rid herself of the paralysing shyness she felt each morning at first meeting. Sharing breakfast with a man, hair shower-damp, cheeks razor-smoothed, movements breath-catching with astringent cologne, was an intimate ritual with which she had not yet come to terms. Each day she promised herself better command, yet each morning her shy reactions prodded the devil in her intuitive companion.

'Did you sleep well?' he asked, their fingers touching as she handed him his cup.

'Perfectly, thank you.' She snatched away her hand, almost spilling the coffee into his lap.

With eyebrows raised he studied her, seeking the reason behind her loss of composure. Elise avoided his interest by scattering a few crumbs upon the floor of the balcony, tempting a small bird nearby into matching bravery.

44

'Pink suits you.' The compliment almost stopped her racing heart. For days she had pandered to his liking for sophisticated, well-dressed women, taking great pains to ensure when wearing the outfits he had bought that gloves matched bag, hairstyle complemented outfit, outfit was appropriate to occasion—not always with conspicuous success. This one small compliment was the first he had ever tendered.

'Aren't you rather flattering your own judgement?' she replied, confused. 'After all, you were the one who insisted I must have this negligée.'

'I was?' He sounded startled at the idea of having shown such a degree of interest. Then he grinned. 'Subconsciously, I must have been remembering that even grubby caterpillars progress eventually towards the beautiful maturity of butterflies' wings.'

After eating he disappeared behind the morning paper, leaving her to her enjoyment of the island's scenery and the less peaceful examination of her own thoughts. Grand'mère, she knew, would be worrying, and that, according to the doctor, was most dangerous to her health. She had sent a letter explaining that she was remaining with Jacques for the time being but would return to the cottage as soon as possible, but the terms in which it had been couched, necessarily evasive, had left huge gaps which the old lady was sure to fill in with notions born of her knowledge of Jacques' reputation. How she longed to be able to slip away, if only for a couple of hours, to quieten her grandmother's fears. But Jacques was as unsettled as quicksilver and too much was at stake to risk letting him out of her sight.

When she sighed he discarded the newspaper and stood up, stretched tall, and flexed his muscles under the warmth of the sun. 'What shall we do today?' he demanded, impatient as a tethered stallion.

Inwardly Elise groaned. Warm sun, peaceful surroundings and most of all, lack of sufficient sleep had combined to make her pleasantly drowsy. 'A picnic?' she suggested hopefully, expecting a quick, derisive refusal.

He surprised her by considering the proposal. 'Do you remember how we used to sail rafts down the Rio Grande?' he grinned. 'Young though you were, you were never scared, in fact, you used to frighten the life out of me by jumping into the river without any warning whenever you felt in need of a swim.'

He so seldom mentioned those earlier days!

With eyes sparkling she leant forward, tiredness forgotten. 'And you were so clever at handling the rafts, even the boatmen admitted you were every bit as expert as they were themselves!'

Deep laughter lines cleft his cheeks, chasing his usual look of bored indifference to the winds. 'How long to get dressed?' he rapped.

'Five minutes!' she gulped, feeling a glow of happiness spreading to the very tips of her toes.

Just two hours later, after flamboyant driving through exotic countryside, along rugged coastline and noble mountain scenery, they reached the east side of the island where a hundred cascading streams poured their waters into the Rio Grande. Immediately they arrived Jacques hired a raft, then after helping her on to it he began with the enthusiasm of a schoolboy truant to navigate the ramshackle-looking craft downstream, propelling and guiding through shallows, then into swifter, deeper water until the raft was buoyant, carried along on a rush of singing water. Years rolled away, everyone but themselves was forgotten as they savoured their return to youth, to the excitement of pitting strength against nature, to the laughing, happy companionship they had once taken so much for granted, to shared glances full of frank enjoyment, to yells of warning, to sudden bouts of soaking spray and even at one stage to a clash of tempers that eventually ended in a fit of loud, undignified merriment.

Beside an isolated clearing on the river bank they made fast the raft before battening down a forest of tall grass to make a couch of cool green. Stretched out under the shade of a huge cotton tree, with spreading branches bearing pods covered with silky down, Jacques accused:

'I'm hungry! I see no sign of the picnic basket you promised.'

Elise rolled over, laughing, reminded of the hint of peevishness the younger Jacques had always displayed whenever his stomach had begun to feel empty. 'Glutton!' she jeered, then dived a hand into her pocket to produce slabs of chocolate and two apples which she hastily held out to appease the vengeful male. The peace-offering was accepted with alacrity and after quenching their thirst with crystal water captured in cupped hands they lay back replete.

'I've loved every minute of today,' she crooned, sucking absently on a wand of molasses grass.

'It isn't over yet,' he rebuked, aggravated by the hint of finality in her tone. 'Why do women find most of their pleasure in retrospect instead of enjoying each moment as it comes? The past hours have *been* enjoyable, the present *is* equally so, but who knows what greater joy might be contained in the hours still to come?' Without warning he moved closer—so quickly he startled a look of apprehension in eyes previously curtained by a sweep of gold-tipped lashes.

The look aroused his anger.

'Let me see if I can guess what is in your mind,' he murmured, bending to brush his lips fractionally across cheeks pink as the petals of mountain pride they had admired on the outward drive. 'You are thinking: "Ah, at last the devil is showing his horns! The gossips were right, I ought to have heeded their warning— *as Camilla did!*"'

His prediction was uncannily accurate; the black-browed antagonist looming over her was a frightening stranger, a wild, unpredictable creature without trace of compassion! She fought an impulse to run from the man who took a perverse delight in underlining his unsuitability as an escort for young, attractive girls by constantly referring to his unsavoury reputation as if it were a canker in his breast.

With the thought came sanity, terror was chased from her mind by the renewed conviction that what she had told her grandmother was true: he needed love and reassurance and most desperately he needed someone who would believe in him and so destroy the myth surrounding his name.

'Cuss-cuss no bore hole a me skin!' she taunted, falling back on the expression they had used often as children—usually after one of their interminable slanging matches—to communicate indifference to harsh words.

A breath rasped in his throat. Unmistakably astonished, he examined laughing eyes, an impudently carefree mouth, a serenely relaxed body that made no attempt to evade his grasp. 'Ghosts can't hurt anyone,' she assured him kindly, ignoring the bands of steel tightening around her arms. 'Past deeds are spectres of another life and as such ought to be either forgotten or ignored.'

'Would that everyone were as charitable!' he grated, gripping her as if longing to test the strength of her glib assurance. 'It is easy to be forgiving of wrong done to others, but what if you should be made to suffer? As you very well may be,' he menaced, 'if ever I should decide to take advantage of your offer to supply *all* of my physical needs!'

With soaring spirits, she discovered that his sting was no longer lethal; not even his threatening hints could disturb her new-found equilibrium. 'Bogeyman!' she scoffed, wriggling easily out of his clutch to stand above him, unaware that the only protection from danger threatening was her own innocent appeal. Unclouded brown eyes smiled down at him as impulsively she held out a helping hand. 'Come on, lazybones, we've idled long enough!'

To his surprise Jacques found himself doing exactly as he was bid!

The return journey was without incident; expertly he manoeuvred the raft, propelling and guiding it through shallows and deep water with complete ease. Each bend of the river revealed views the same yet different; troubled thought was easily dispersed by such surrounding beauty as ackee trees holding decorative clusters of bright red fruits; the glorious yellow blossom of the ebony tree and tall palms with trunks shooting sky high under an umbrella of swaying fronds. They had brought swimsuits, so in a pool of placid water they stopped to swim, emulating seals cavorting in the water, before blissfully stretching out on the raft to dry in the sunshine.

Trees carry neither clocks nor calendars, so when eventually they returned the raft to a boatman the sun was already low on the horizon and by the time they reached their hotel after the long drive across the island it had long since set. Elise was laughing when they entered the hotel foyer, so engrossed in Jacques' amusing conversation she did not hear her name called as they sauntered towards the lift.

'Miss Portland!' The second call was penetrating in its urgency. Immediately, she and Jacques swung round and were confronted by a coldly angry doctor who made no attempt to hide his contempt of them both. 'Where the devil have you been?' he charged. 'I've had boys searching for you all over the island since early morning! I had hoped you might turn up at Madame Calvet's of you own accord, but obviously you rate pleasure higher than any misgivings you might have felt about your grand-mother's health!'

The shocking attack took Elise by surprise, eras-ing in a second her carefree expression. 'Has some-thing happened?' She grabbed his arm, her eyes showing dark against suddenly pale cheeks. 'Tell me!' she shook him in her agitation, 'is something wrong with Grand'mère?'

His mouth relaxed slightly, but his voice retained its tone of censure. 'Mattie called me first thing this morning. Your grandmother has suffered another stroke—more serious than the others—and she is asking for you. I'm going back to the cottage now, if you'd like to accompany me we might just be in time ...' A harsh sob tore from Elise's throat. She was stricken, of that there was no doubt, and his attitude softened. Examining his watch, he offered, 'I'll wait just five minutes longer ...' before turn-ing to stride away.

'Don't bother, *docteur*, I'll take her! Please do not delay further, Madame Calvet may be in need of your attention.' Elise hardly recognised the authoritative voice. Jacques seldom reacted with feeling—more often than not an indolent shrug was his only return against any aggravating situation—but this time he had obviously decided to take com-mand.

The doctor's nostrils flared, but he did not wait to argue. 'Good,' he agreed crisply, 'then I'll be on my way.'

In her numbed state, Elise was grateful to obey Jacques' instructions to have a quick shower and to change into something warm enough to counter the night breezes. Another long drive lay ahead of them and she had no wish to arrive at her grand-mother's bedside too chilled to be of use. But he could not persuade her to take food—even a cupful of soup would choke her, she assured him—so five minutes later they were again tearing along the quiet roads at a speed which in other circumstances would have caused her fear.

He made no attempt to comfort with words, and for that she was grateful. Guilt was gnawing at her conscience. For two weeks she had all but ignored the existence of the old lady to whom she owed everything, and now she felt she was reaping retri-bution for her selfish, uncaring attitude.

Jacques' features were sombre as he drove swift-ly but superbly well along the mountain roads, and his silent sharing of her burden was comforting. He, too, cared deeply for her grandmother. During his boyhood she had been the only female influence in his life and to her he had homed instinctively whenever he felt in need of the warmth and under-standing unhappily absent in a household predomin-antly male. Elise found herself remembering the hours of discussion that had taken place in the cot-tage whenever she, Jacques and her grandmother had been imprisoned indoors by occasional winter rain. They had sat around a fire—a novelty because it was so seldom lit—he and her grandmother deep in conversation, exchanging views that went far above her childish understanding. To her, he had of-ten sounded pompous, but her grandmother had never betrayed amusement, rather she had heard him out before gently guiding his opinions towards

52

a more moderate viewpoint. Yes, he had certainly loved her! Had he not said once with all the passion of deprived boyhood: 'I'll always regard you as a mother, *madame*, you have been kind enough to allow me to share your home, your hospitality, your understanding. Some day I hope in some small measure to be able to repay your many acts of kindness.'

She stirred, easing her stiff limbs, and he commented wryly, 'Not the most perfect ending to our day.'

'Then you were happy, too?' she questioned eagerly, sensing a return of earlier magic.

'Happy?' he considered carefully. 'What is happiness? So often people hanker after pleasure, wanting more than their fair share, and finish up more miserable than those who are burdened with care.'

'Then you didn't enjoy our outing.' She slumped back into her seat, hurt by his cynicism.

'I didn't say that,' he corrected, delving into an inside pocket in search of a cigar. He waited until she had served him with a light before adding the laconic aside, 'The day has not been without its compensations—but every sweet has its sour just as every evil its good.'

Mattie was waiting in the doorway when their car drew up in front of the cottage. Her cheeks were streaked with tears as she ushered them inside then motioned them upstairs, too overcome with grief to even pretend an answer to Elise's urgent: 'How is she?'

Her grandmother lay still and white beneath cool sheets, but as they tiptoed across to the bed her eyelids lifted and a faint smile traced colourless lips. 'You have arrived, *ma petite*, now I am content ...' she breathed. Her glance rested upon Jacques, a silent shadow, and momentarily she betrayed a flicker of distress, but then, as his eyes steadily held hers, serenity spread across her features, a look of infinite peace. 'Bless you both, *mes enfants*,' she whispered, then lapsed once more into sleep.

Elise sat with her all during the night, holding her hand, whispering words of remorse and promises of future consideration to the old lady who seemed too tired to make any effort to respond. Just before dawn she rallied and surprised her with the penetrating whisper. 'Where is Jacques, I must speak with him ...?'

'He's downstairs, I'll go and fetch him, Grand'-mère,' she offered eagerly, overjoyed by the suggestion of returning strength. She jumped to her feet, but a weak gesture bid her stay.

'I wish to speak to him ... alone, *chérie* ... You must rest ...'

'Nonsense!' Elise smiled through a rush of relieved tears, 'I'm as strong as a horse, you know that, Grand'mère. But I wouldn't mind a cup of tea, so I'll stay downstairs long enough for you to have your little chat.'

Jacques was in the kitchen trying to console Mattie, but when Elise imparted the good news that her grandmother seemed much improved neither face brightened even fractionally. In fact, Mattie began weeping even more copiously.

'That's enough, Mattie,' Jacques ordered curtly,

'you'll make yourself ill. Try to coax Elise to eat while I'm upstairs, she's had hardly anything all day and no doubt she'll insist upon returning to sit with her grandmother for what remains of the night.'

'I believe you're right.' Elise smiled for the first time since her arrival. 'I do feel quite ravenous now.'

When he disappeared upstairs she relaxed in her seat with a weary yawn and watched Mattie bustling around the stove preparing a meal. Overtried emotions had weakened her, but her tired body was buoyed up with renewed hope and quite happily she set upon the meal Mattie had prepared, communicating her optimism to the doleful old servant as she ate.

'She looked very much brighter when she awoke,' she assured her, 'more alert and quite determined to speak to Jacques. She's very fond of him really.' She pushed away her plate and nodded acceptance of a second cup of tea. 'Although she may have felt some reservations because of the gossip, nothing can alter the fact that they have always been extremely fond of each other and—'

She stopped short. Mattie was not listening, she was staring in front of her, her eyes reflecting dread. Elise swung around and saw Jacques standing still and grave in the doorway.

'Elise, *ma petite*,' he held out his arms as if offering shelter, 'it's all over . . . your grand'mère is dead.'

CHAPTER FIVE

THE cottage looked the same, but the heart had gone from it. Silence filled rooms that once had seemed too tiny to contain the noise of happy voices, childish laughter and Mattie's unmelodious voice chanting never-ending calypsos. Not even the sound of pans banging down upon the stove issued from the kitchen—Mattie had disappeared after the funeral and would be alone somewhere nursing her grief for the rest of the day.

Elise settled her head back against a scarlet cushion, her face stark against the brilliant backcloth. She did not feel like talking, yet so much was waiting to be said. Clenching her knuckles hard, she took the initiative. 'I had not thought of it until recently, but I suppose you, Jacques, were Grand'mère's landlord. Will you allow me to renew the lease,' she laughed nervously, 'or shall I have to find somewhere else to live?'

The morose figure sitting in the shadows stirred impatiently. Her grandmother's death had affected him strangely; for days he had been moody, speaking only when necessary and even then with pre-occupation, as if some problem lay heavily on his mind. She waited, expecting assurances that the cottage was hers for as long as she wanted it, then was shocked by his abruptly imparted decision. 'This cottage will never be re-let during my lifetime, it will remain as it is—as it has always been ...!' He broke off, drifting back to his all-important, *excluding* thoughts.

Elise felt choking fear. If he would not allow her to live in the cottage where was she to go? There was no money—her grandmother had left surprisingly little, enough merely to cover the funeral expenses—and her bits of furniture, although dearly loved, would fetch only pence on the open market. A job! Perhaps she might manage to find work in the capital—in a hotel where she could live in.

She stood up and with heartbreaking dignity intruded once more upon his study. 'Would ... would you consider employing Mattie?' she pleaded. 'I know she's old, but you know how well she cooks —remember how fond you are of her stuffed baked yams?'

'Baked yams?' he repeated absently, catching only the end of the sentence.

Elise began pacing about, knowing she was on the verge of shedding the tears everyone had urged her to shed but which up until now she had found impossible. Strange, she thought, rubbing perspiration from her palms, how immeasurable grief had not broken her control, yet one slight from an uncaring man was threatening to break her heart!

'How long before I have to move out?' she cried, unable to stand another second of uncertainty.

For once, it seemed, she had got through to him. His head jerked up, her torment shocking in its impact. With an oath he jerked from his chair and strode forward, catching her by the shoulders as she tried to turn away.

'Little fool!' he derided, angry with himself, but

57

flaying her. 'You can move out immediately,' he lashed. Then taking pity, he spelled out gently, 'You are moving into the Grand House with me. Mattie will come too, initially to act as chaperone, then once we are married she can take charge of the kitchen and perhaps create order out of the existing chaos.'

Silently he waited while Elise digested his devastating words. Her head was bowed so that a curtain of brown hair obscured expressions of incredulity, relief and joy. Impatiently he shook her. 'Well, have you nothing to say? Have I the great fortune of having chosen a bride who will remain dumb?'

She collapsed against him, laughing, then seconds later began to sob. He made light of everything; it was not really so surprising that he had made no mention of love. He was autocratic—therefore he would consider a proposal unnecessary. Thoughtlessness would account for his not having assured her earlier that her future was safe and even as a boy he had been undemonstrative, conditioned from childhood to displaying a stiff upper lip, to showing no emotion, to burying feelings of tenderness lest he should appear any less of a man! Knowing him as she did, she should know better than to feel deprived at the lack of a betrothal kiss!

Nevertheless, she chanced a rebuff. 'Are you certain that what you feel is not just pity, you really *do* want to marry me?'

Before releasing her he brushed his lips across her childish brow. 'Pity? Why should I feel pity, have I not enough troubles of my own?' he quizzed inscrutably before moving across to the window, putting the width of the room between them, leaving her stranded on a sea of heaving carpet.

Later, Jeremy Sherlock called to check that Elise was sleeping properly and offered to supply a mild sedative once he had studied her distrait face and heavy eyes. For once, it seemed, he was human enough to understand that mental torment far exceeded the pain of the physical, so he did not press her when she brushed aside his offer with the question, 'Has a medication yet been devised to relieve heartache or self-reproach? I would welcome any pill that could ease the torment of knowing I helped to kill Grand'mère. I *worried* her to her death!' she flung bitterly, 'and if you're here to reproach me then you're wasting your time because no criticism of yours could be any more bitter than my own!'

She was standing with her back to him, looking vacantly towards the horizon where sea and sky were distinguishable only by different shadings of blue. He joined her at the window, standing close but not touching. 'Your grandmother often told me what a comfort you were to her, how much she admired your independence and youthful common sense. If you're thinking that those weeks you spent with the Comte caused her worry, then forget it. She never doubted your integrity for one moment and neither, strangely enough, did she doubt his!'

Her relief was tremendous, but even the gratitude she felt was not proof against his surprised inflection when he admitted that Jacques had shared her grandmother's trust. 'You dislike Jacques,

59

don't you? Could it be that you are one of those people who instinctively resent anyone born to position and wealth?'

His quiet answer reached across her shoulder, frank and completely unashamed. 'As we seem to be in the mood for baring souls, I'll admit to a feeling of animosity—not because of his wealth or position,' he hastened to add, 'but because of his casual handling of the affections of someone I hold very dear. Camilla's heart was in the palm of his hand,' he charged bitterly, 'their tempestuous affair was the talk of the island, yet emotionally he kept her dangling, so uncertain of his feelings she was driven to delivering a sort of ultimatum by accepting the offer of a cruise in the hope that the threat of separation would bring him to his senses. How will she react, I wonder,' his tone took on an abrasive quality Elise recognized as pain, 'when she returns next week to learn how quickly he's consoled himself with you?'

Too shocked to face him, she kept her back turned as she whispered, 'How do you know all this? How can you be sure . . . ?'

She winced from his humourless laughter. 'Camilla sees me as a father-confessor. One of the drawbacks of my profession is that many people expect doctors to be as celibate as priests and refuse to accept that we're as vulnerable to love as other men. I make no apologies for repeating what she told me in confidence because I would do anything to spare her pain. I hate to admit it, but she and Jacques will never find happiness apart. *I* have accepted that fact,' he accused hoarsely, all the while looking right at her, 'so why can't you?'

Elise had no idea when he left. Hours afterwards she was still standing where he had left her, tussling with her conscience, denying an inward voice that was insisting that Jacques must be told the truth. Fate had seen fit to disrupt their lives with one cruel twist of timing. If Jacques had decided only hours earlier to propose to Camilla he would not have arrived at Port Royal just in time to see the yacht leave harbour. If, on the other hand, Camilla had remained on the island just a few hours longer she would by now be preparing a bridal trousseau fit for a *comtesse*. So many confusing ifs and buts!

There was only one thing of which she was certain. Jacques had never really loved Camilla; the past weeks she had spent in his company had convinced her that Camilla's attraction for him was as abstract as that of a beautiful flower and would as quickly fade. At this very moment he was out making arrangements for a quiet ceremony to be accomplished so swiftly it would be over days before the yacht returned. Dared she allow the arrangements to continue knowing Camilla was on her way back to the island hoping to surprise a proposal from the man whose ultra-sensitivity had led him to believe that gossip had driven her away? Camilla was *wrong* for him! It would be hard, *but not impossible*, to ignore all else and let the wedding take place as planned!

She and Mattie moved into the Grand House that night. As Jacques drove the car between two lodges the main block loomed up ahead, a great cliff of buttery stone, heavily decorated and rusticated, with tall windows slashed through stone to throw light into an immense inner hall. A proud, disdainful house, elegant, but retaining some of the coldness of the aristocratic Montagues.

Nervously she stepped across the threshold, sensing a battery of eyes staring down from a gallery hung with ancestral portraits. Never before had she set foot inside the Grand House; the old Comte had jealously guarded his privacy and child visitors had not been welcome.

Jacques instructed, 'Go below stairs, will you, Mattie, and muster some of the servants? Ask whoever's in charge to show you which rooms you are to use, then see about getting us some food.'

'A sure nuff will, Massa Jacques—sir— Comte ...' Her black face was a picture of puzzlement as she struggled to think of the correct form of address for someone who had in the past received many a ticking off for his impudence but who now, in his own surroundings, seemed to merit a curtsy.

'Master Jacques will do.' As his mouth relaxed into a smile the sudden transformation left Elise shaken. For days he had remained aloof and distant, speaking only in curt monosyllables.

When Mattie left them Elise felt he was at a loss to know what to do with her. Embarrassment made her awkward, so when he suggested moving into the small salon she accepted with alacrity, her heels clicking across the black and white checked marble floor, past an elegant staircase curving downward with the sweep of a duchess's train, until finally she reached the door he had indicated.

Hopeful of finding comfort, she hastened inside, then faltered, catching her breath at the sight of richly brocaded chairs with curved gilt legs, inlaid tables set uniformly against walls furnished stark white so as to provide impact for costly vases, priceless pictures and other objets d'art scattered around the room. A highly polished floor scattered with jewel-coloured rugs and a high painted ceiling underlined the stiff formality of the room.

Feeling dwarfed by such magnificence, she pleaded, 'Isn't there somewhere smaller?'

'I'm afraid not, nothing even remotely as comfortable as your grand'mère's home,' he confessed with a shrug. 'Why else do you suppose I subjected you both to such prolonged visits? My grandfather was a man of spartan tastes, he loved beautiful things but frowned upon too obvious comfort. As you can see,' he flung his arms wide, 'the house cries out for a woman's touch. You have my permission to change anything you wish, and if you do manage to transform it into anything resembling a real home I shall feel unexpectedly rewarded.'

Unexpectedly rewarded! All night long as she tossed and turned in an unfamiliar bed the two words illuminated her mind with the insistency of a neon sign. The term seemed to imply some form of sacrifice, unanticipated compensation for some deed which initially he had considered profitless. Elise winced from the thought that he might merit marriage to her just such a deed. She had far more to offer than the services of a housekeeper—sympathy, understanding and an abundance of love were qualities prized far higher than mere bodily comforts by the majority of men. But Jacques could not be measured by the same yardstick as other men, his unpredictable actions set him apart from the rest, and as for guessing his motives ... She slid out of bed and knelt down to pray. The wedding had been arranged to take place in two days' time and she needed strength to help her carry out her decision to remain silent, a decision taken not for her own sake but for his!

She spent the following forty-eight hours in an agony of indecision. Twice she found herself on the verge of contacting Jeremy Sherlock, experiencing a morbid desire to punish herself by talking further about Camilla's feelings for Jacques and the possible outcome of a reunion uncomplicated by outside influences. But each time she held back, telling herself that any opinion of Jeremy's was bound to be biased in favour of Camilla. His was an undemanding, selfless love, she sensed with quick shame, but he would be ruthless, nevertheless, towards anyone who might threaten the happiness of the girl he adored.

News of the forthcoming wedding, together with the new duties imposed, had helped to relieve some of Mattie's grief. She had even begun to hum a little as she went about her work and the rebukes piled upon the heads of servants grown idle in the employ of an uncaring master often had edges blunted by the beginnings of a smile. Elise found her in the kitchen when, unable to tolerate further solitary thought, she went in search of company.

'Something smells good!' she greeted cheerfully, perching on the edge of a well-scrubbed table. What's for dinner?'

'Pepperpot soup, roast duck with banana stuffing, an' matrimony to follow,' Mattie supplied, her black eyes still not quite ready to sparkle. Matrimony—pulped star-apple mixed with pieces of orange and a dash of sherry—had been a favourite sweet of her grandmother's and for a moment Elise was poignantly reminded of her loss. Quickly, Mattie attempted to cover up her lapse by changing the subject. With a furtive glance around to make sure no one was within earshot, she whispered: D'you wanna see the obeah man, Missie Elise? A' knows somebody who kin fetch him.'

Elise stared blankly, then as realization dawned she coloured and rebuked sharply, 'Don't be ridiculous, Mattie! How many times did Grand'mère warn you about believing in such superstitious nonsense, as well as reminding you that the practice of obeah is illegal? No one is allowed to accept money any more for casting so-called spells—and anyway, what makes you think I'm in need of such a service?'

Mattie weathered her indignation with infuriating calm, needing no guidance other than the sight of a woebegone mouth and constantly wrinkled brow to confirm her suspicion that all was not well between the bridal pair. Mebbe obeah man no good fer curin' sickness no more,' she admitted cautiously, 'but he's still plenty good at mendin' bust-ups and his love potions sure nuff work fast. Why, only last week . . .'

'I don't want to know, Mattie!' Elise slid from the table and made towards the door, her cheeks burning. All during childhood she had listened to Mattie's tales about the obeah man who could cure all ills, both of mind and body, with his miraculous potions—even inflicting ills upon one's enemies if the price were right! Her indignation had its basis in shame, because deep down she was as superstitious as the islanders and had even toyed with the idea of using the existing underground movement to make contact with the man who, his followers decreed, could revive a fading love, assuage a broken heart and even, with the help of a love potion, capture the heart of a loved one—however disinterestd!

Appalled by her own naïveté, she sped along the passageways in the direction of her room, oblivious of the man standing in the hall who winced at the sound of rubber-shod feet slapping against priceless marble floors and the consequent echoes bouncing from a finely sculptured ceiling.

She was not aware that he had followed her until he made his presence known by calling her by name. By that time her speed had slackened and she was sauntering along a landing lined with glass-fronted cabinets housing a collection of fine china. She was admiring the design of a fantastic tulip vase when his voice scythed across her shoulder, startling her so much she spun round to face him.

'Jacques, what a pleasant surprise! I understood when you left after breakfast that you'd be gone all day. Perhaps we could have lunch together—if you're not too busy, that is?' she faltered, nonplussed by his frown.

'I've already eaten,' he informed her, his hard glance travelling downward, taking in windswept hair tied back with a shoe-lace, tip-tilted nose, sunburnt and freckled, her usual garb of washed-out shirt and shrunken jeans, then lastly the offending shoes, once white but now a disreputable grey. Her enquiring look seemed to disconcert him as he sought for words to express his dissatisfaction without unnecessary wounding, but after a prolonged silence during which her puzzlement grew more and more obvious he gave a very Gallic shrug of despair.

'What age are you?' he clenched.

Her lips fell open with surprise. 'I'm nineteen, of course! Don't tell me you've forgotten that there's six years between us, you reminded me of it often enough when we were children!'

'*Mon Dieu!*' he muttered. 'I must have spanned a lifetime since that time! Whereas you,' his downward glance was unkind, 'seem to be taking far too long to grow up. Most girls of nineteen strive to emulate their elder sisters by copying their style of dress and sophisticated outlook, yet you are at your happiest dressed like a scruffy beachcomber! You have plenty of suitable clothes, so why not wear them? Tomorrow morning you are to become the Comtesse de Montague——I sincerely hope that once we are married I'll be able to rely upon your good sense not to appear in public, or anywhere else for that matter, in the disreputable form of dress you now favour. Run along,' he shrugged as if the sight of her made him irritable, 'try a different hairstyle, try something, *anything*, that will help to chase

67

the dew of infancy from your face! Remember also,' he stressed grimly, 'that tomorrow I'll expect to see you changed. I refuse absolutely to take as my bride a ruffian with sand in her shoes and fruit juice smeared across her face!'

He strode off, leaving her gaping. Then when the sound of his footsteps faded into silence she rushed to her room at a furious pace, banging the door behind her in temper. Rebelliously, she stared at her reflection in a mirror. True, she was not exactly a fashion plate, but neither was she *scruffy*, nor a *beachcomber*! And what was so upsetting about a little fruit juice? No one could eat mango without smearing— Her thoughts screeched to a halt as suddenly she recalled the many hours of tuition expended by her teachers on just such items of social behaviour. Feeling quick shame, she forced herself to admit that his accusations were not entirely unjustified; he preferred his companions to be svelte and dignified, a complement to his own impeccable taste. Even Grand'mère, she recalled sadly, had urged in a much less brutal manner for some sign of return for all the money invested in her expensive education.

Savagely, she tugged away the bootlace, allowing silken brown tresses to ripple past her shoulders. Thoughtfully she assessed her potential, finding encouragement in fine bone structure, glowing skin and eyes brown and soft as the petals of a pansy. Her figure was good, she judged, kicking her way out of the rough jeans Jacques abominated, and her legs were excellent—far better than Camilla's, whose ankles were a little too thick . . .

thick ...

Impulsively, a decision was made. Elise ran into the bathroom and muttered fiercely under her breath as she prepared to take a shower, 'I'll show him! I'll show them all, Grand'mère, that your efforts to turn me into a lady have not been in vain. He'll have cause to feel proud of me yet!

CHAPTER SIX

THE wedding took place in a private chapel attached to the Grand House. Pillars of Italian marble supported a ceiling of exquisitely carved and latticed wood. A cornice of plaster cherubs fringed delicately frescoed walls and a marble floor and pews of polished oak gained added beauty from shafts of coloured sunshine playing through stained-glass windows. Behind a font, brought into service for every Montague christening, was a statue of the Madonna and Child and six steps, richly carpeted, led up to an altar hung with tapestries embroidered with gold thread. Candles thick as a man's wrist towered from gold bases and from their lighted wicks thin streams of pungent blue smoke wreathed, mingling with the perfume of lilies and honeysuckle amassed in huge vases—a sharp, breathtaking scent Elise was ever afterwards to associate with apprehension and awe.

Jacques was waiting in the chapel when she arrived on the arm of his lawyer, Monsieur Martre, who, together with Mattie, had been imposed upon to act as witnesses. An officiating padre and an unseen organist made up a total congregation of six—not even the servants were aware of the wedding taking place in their midst.

Elise began to tremble as she walked up the aisle. Jacques was standing face forward and when, at her appearance, the organist struck up the wedding march, he jerked erect as if the signal had reacted upon a sensitive nerve.

'Have courage, *ma petite*,' Monsieur Martre squeezed her hand and beamed down at her, thinking himself fortunate to be escorting one of the loveliest brides he had ever seen. Though her dress was short and simple in design, the white material clung, giving enchanting glimpses of petite curves. Brown hair, full of trapped sunlight, caressed the pale oval of her face, a stray wisp of hair falling down upon her forehead worrying to her, but the man at her side saw it as the small imperfection necessary to bring into focus her innocent beauty. A mantilla of white lace filched from one of the many treasure chests stored about the house did duty as a veil, a symbol of purity complemented by long lashes resting on faintly flushed cheeks, and a pulse that ran riot immediately Jacques took her hand.

'Cynical dog!' Monsieur Martre thought as he relinquished his charge. 'What sort of man is he to be able to look so indifferently upon such a bride?'

But Elise was not dismayed, only she was near enough to notice blue eyes flashing surprise an instant before shutters were drawn and though she dared not turn to look, she felt certain as the service progressed that a smile had begun to curl upon lips which earlier had been grim.

His responses contrasted cold and clear against her breathless efforts, but the padre was kind and guided her gently when she stumbled over traditional phrases.

'With my body I thee worship!' Why, when it

was so true, should it be so hard for her to say?

'Till death us do part!' When Jacques glanced her way she controlled a wayward sob, wondering if his promises were given lightly or if, like hers, they were for ever and a day.

The ring felt cold as it was slid upon her finger, then changed to a band of fire when instead of releasing her he tightened his grasp. 'Well, how does it feel to be Madame la Comtesse?' he quizzed with desperate lightness, looking, she thought, as if he had just said a last goodbye. Foreboding shuddered through her, but she managed an incoherent reply. The enormity of her deceit seemed, within the sanctity of the chapel, to have assumed gigantic proportions. By remaining silent she had deprived him of his right to choose. Blindly, she had convinced herself that what mattered most was his need of love, the right kind of love—*her kind!* But what if she had misjudged the man who was a complete antithesis of the boy he had once been? Already, she knew that in anger he could be terrible —was she ever to know the sweet tempest of his love?

After the service, at Jacques' polite insistence, Monsieur Martre retired with them to the library to share a solitary bottle of champagne, but upon sensing that Jacques was finding his small talk tedious he offered a final toast to their future happiness then said his goodbyes.

'Why were you so abrupt?' Elise demanded, embarrassed by his lack of courtesy.

'The man is a bore, and I refuse to tolerate being bored,' he drawled, making only half an effort to

72

smother a yawn. Monsieur Martre had tried his polite best to ease a situation made difficult by Jacques' moodiness; his criticism made her angry.

'It's the peculiarity of a bore that he's the last person to find himself out!' she accused. 'Your behaviour was not exactly conducive to sparkling conversation and witty repartee!'

She was appalled when he turned on her savagely. 'I don't feel particularly sparkling, nor do I feel witty, so for God's sake put on your sandshoes and run along and play!'

She blinked. For the past hour Jacques had been simmering, nursing some resentment that would give his mind no peace; her criticism had added fuel to the flame!

She had the good sense to remain silent as he began prowling, pacing the floor as arrogantly as his pirate ancestors must have paced the deck, ready, willing even, for some adversary to unsheath his sword. Pirate blood had been diluted from the Montague stream throughout generations of marriage, but every now and then a rebel emerged, a throw-back to the first filibustering founder of the line. Elise was quick to recognize the resentment holding him in sway—like the first sea hawk ever to be captured, he was thrashing against chains that threatened the freedom of flying wings!

Dully, she faced the fact that whatever the reason behind his offer of marriage it was not love; obviously he was already regretting his impulsive action. Calling upon great reserves of courage, she asked, 'Why did you marry me, Jacques? Please,' she went on swiftly when he spun round to protest, 'don't pretend, don't lie to me. You think me a simple-minded child, gauche and immature, but I'm not a child, I'm a woman, one intuitive enough to realize that already you're regarding our marriage as a terrible mistake!'

She ought to have waited until the devil driving him had been calmed; in his present mood her quiet pleas would seem to him to ring with reproach.

'Predictably, his answer was coldly cruel. 'I was thinking primarily of duty to family; I need the stability of my own home, my own wife—a docile, *available* wife,' he stressed. 'In the past I've taken advantage of many women who were eager to satisfy my needs, but mistresses can be dangerous—especially if they happen to be other men's wives—and also they are unnecessarily expensive. Marriage to you seemed an ideal solution—not only did it resolve my own problem, it was a way of keeping the promise I made to your grandmother.'

'Promise?' Elise echoed faintly, staring at him as if she were seeing him for the first time.

'Just before she died she asked me to look after you and I promised her I would.' He shrugged. 'Considering her many acts of kindness I felt it was the least I could do.'

Something precious within her died, killed by his callous confession. She stared at him, hurt beyond expression, and before his indifferent eyes the child he despised became a woman, a hurt, humiliated woman mourning the loss of a cherished dream.

Then a shaft of white-hot anger speared her

numbness, activating the spirited reply, 'You're quite right, it *was* the least you could do—I doubt if even you could have done less!' Aggravated further by the haughty tilt of his head, she cried out, 'I wish now that I'd told you why Camilla left the island—I might at least have saved myself from the humiliation of marriage to a man whose chief requirements would seem to be a cheap mistress and a cloak of respectability!'

He strode forward to grab her by the shoulders. 'What knowledge do you have of Camilla's plans?'

She experienced a mixture of triumph and terror when she saw how deeply she had scored, then felt pain when in his frustration he shook her fiercely. '*Tell me!* I demand to know!'

'She planned to spur you on to a proposal,' she gasped. 'She's in love with you, and as you didn't seem to be responding she accepted the offer of a cruise hoping the separation would bring you up to scratch. Unfortunately for me,' she stressed bitterly, 'she left a little too early, not knowing you'd decided to do exactly as she wished!'

'You were aware of this!' he hissed, 'yet you let me continue with the ceremony, allowed me to go on thinking I had been rejected by the woman I love! *Sacrée mère de Dieu!*' he blasphemed, 'I could kill you for that!' In his passion his hands closed around her throat and for terrifying seconds she fought for breath as his grip tightened. 'How did you come by this information? Not from Camilla herself?'

'Jeremy Sherlock told me ...' The confession was almost choked out of her. 'Camilla confided in him

75

just before she left.' She stared at him in fear.

It was a relief to feel the pressure of his hands relax, but a relief shortlived once she met his eyes full of condemning hate. A wave of nausea overwhelmed her when he stepped back to accuse in a voice tight with dislike, 'So, once again you have schemed successfully to get your own way! You must think yourself very clever, but I promise you this, *comtesse*,' he hissed in his anger, 'for as long as you live you will rue this day!'

Elise's punishment began that night when without knocking he strode into her bedroom. 'We will dine out this evening,' he commanded, ignoring visible signs of weeping. 'All of Kingston is waiting to congratulate me, so I've booked a table at the Sirocco where most of my friends congregate. You will go on show to a critical audience,' he scoffed with eyes of flint. 'They will be expecting much in the way of glamour—too bad they are going to be disappointed.'

'I . . . can't, not tonight. I have a headache . . .'

Her panic-stricken expression left him unmoved. 'You must,' he decreed with such piratical arrogance that she recognized at once the futility of opposing his will—even if he had to resort to slinging her across his shoulder in the manner of his ancestors. with some unwilling female plunder, she would be made to obey.

She mustered her tattered pride. 'Very well, I'll get ready.'

There were plenty of dresses suitable to her role of mistress, she decided bitterly as she selected from her wardrobe some of the items Jacques had bought in defiance of her own stated dislike of way-out design. Most of them she had sworn never to wear, but slinky materials designed to sculpt every curve, with tops slashed in deep vees almost to the waist, seemed to fit perfectly the part she had been designated to play. A mistress he wanted and a mistress he should have, she thought, so mortally hurt she was immune to reason.

The dress she finally chose was saffron yellow, a kaftan of see-through silk chiffon, hand-embroidered with sequins and diamonds. A choker of yellow gems supported a ruby pendant that dived downwards between her breasts, following the line of a cleavage slit almost to the navel. Lavishly applied lipstick in a deep purple shade added wantonness to a defiant mouth and nail varnish of a matching colour gave to once-capable hands the look of feline claws. False eyelashes, eyeliner, eyeshadow, mascara—every known aid to feminine allure was made use of skilfully, as she had been taught, until finally she rose from the dressing table satisfied that she would outdo even the most sensational of Jacques' female acquaintances.

She received only the most cursory of looks as he handed her into the car, and during the drive to the capital she remained silent, huddled into the wrap that so far had blunted the full impact of her appearance. When they entered the hotel foyer she made a hasty excuse and left him to fume quietly while she hurried to the cloakroom.

Even within the ultra-sophisticated capital's most popular night-spot, where way-out dress barely merited a glance, they were not quite immune to shock. Calmly, Elise discarded her wrap and ran the gauntlet of amazed gasps and wide stares from women wildly envious of her daring. She surprised herself by feeling nothing, neither shame nor discomfort, as she repaired an already flawless complexion with hands perfectly steady before sweeping into the foyer with the poised aplomb of a born *comtesse*.

Jacques was still standing where she had left him, and as Elise advanced her numbed feelings reacted to the sight of broad shoulders outlined by a white dinner jacket and a darkly satanic profile with eyes so compelling they could coax honey from the tightest bud. Instinct, or it might have been the fixed attention of people staring past him, set him swinging on his heel just when she was within a few paces. She wanted to laugh aloud at his incredulous expression, but instead slipped her hand into the crook of his arm and encouraged with a glint of mockery, 'Shall we go in?'

As expected, he rallied admirably, displaying an imperturbable front to the gathering of spectators, but beneath her hand she felt him tense, a warning that later she would reap the consequences of her impulsive action. Under cover of conversation he bent down and as he helped her into a seat at their table whispered savagely, 'Shouldn't you have worn something under that dress?'

Again laughter bubbled up inside her. She had not really thought she could go through with it, had even had visions of panicking at the last moment and having to run, but now that she had disconcerted the imperturbable Comte she was beginning to enjoy herself!

Before hundreds of curious eyes she lifted her hand to caress his cheek, her glance projecting the adoration of a loving bride. 'You bought this dress, remember?' she murmured, a wicked dimple playing at the corner of her mouth, 'and all well-dressed mistresses are wearing see-throughs these days!'

He sat down opposite, freezing with a stare the glance of a hovering waiter whose eyes kept straying towards tantalizing curves showing milk-white through golden mist. Knowing herself safe in the midst of a crowd, Elise relaxed. Many covert glances were being cast towards their table and many hands waved a greeting, but their owners were obviously allowing them time to order their meal before intruding with requests for introductions. But his curt acknowledgements were barely encouraging, and as soon as they had made their choice from the menu he rose and almost ordered her on to the dance-floor. 'Certainly, I'd love to dance, darling!' she teased for the benefit of nearby eavesdroppers, floating past him in a diaphanous yellow cloud, leaving the scent of jasmine drifting in her wake.

The band was in a mellow mood, the music unashamedly sentimental, and under lowered lights she slipped into his arms as if she had been there many times before. She felt him stiffen as she nestled close and smiled to herself, understanding why. He was a virile man, very receptive to female advances, but she was advancing too fast to allow his preconceived notions of her immaturity to adjust!

Bound to keep up the pretence of besotted bridegroom, he held her close, his lips resting against the smooth sweep of her brow, but for all his apparent control his voice sounded strangled when he accused in an undertone, 'What do you hope to achieve by appearing in public dressed like a harlot? Are you enjoying having every man in the room looking—*leering*—hoping at any minute to see exposed what little you have left to the imagination? And as for all that warpaint, I've half a mind,' he gritted, 'to march you to the nearest fountain and scrub it off!'

'Don't you dare!' Her head jerked up, alarmed by his expression of intent. She had expected surprise, even scorn, but for some reason he was coldly, intensely *furious*!

Hoping to appease, she pleaded, 'You doubted my ability to appear sophisticated, you accused me of extreme youth, then almost in the same breath you informed me that you married me to gain a mistress. Yet because I have attempted to correct those faults you flay me with condemnation. Do you know what you *do* want, Jacques?'

Forgetting the role they had to play, she pulled away to glare at him, challenging him for an answer, but he jerked her back into his arms. Too angry to argue, he guided her around the floor, his hands, though resting lightly, burning through the flimsy material of her dress. His breathing was uneven and the angle of his jaw set rigid, indicating inner turbulence. Wild hope soared. Could it possibly be that for all his bitter words he was finding her attractive?

Light as air, she teased, 'In the Grand House

there are many pictures of nude ladies permanently on display—if you're so prudish why don't you have them removed?'

Only to be immediately deflated by the terse reply, 'To be nude is to be beautiful—to be undressed is merely to be vulgar!'

CHAPTER SEVEN

ELISE was not altogether unprepared when Jacques steered her towards the exit with the tight-lipped command, 'We're leaving, wait here while I send someone to fetch your wrap.' With cheeks aflame, she remained on the spot he had chosen, a quiet corner partially screened by a display of flowers and potted palms. Keeping her back turned on late diners spilling through the entrance into the foyer, she brushed hasty fingers across lashes beaded with tears, so conscious of her humiliation she was deaf to sounds of laughing, happy voices echoing all around her.

Inwardly, she was raging against her own lack of spirit; to give in without a fight was fatal, especially when the antagonist was one of Jacques' calibre, but the alternative would have been to create a scene and that was unthinkable. Her heart raced as another possibility presented itself: what if she were to return to their table in his absence? That way he would be forced to join her or else risk the speculation his absence would be bound to incur!

The decision made, she spun round, anxious to carry out the plan before courage deserted her, and after checking that he was nowhere in sight she began making in the direction of the dining-room, sidestepping groups of chatting people as she progressed rapidly, glancing around every now and then to make sure Jacques was not striding in pursuit. Her heart was thumping, her mouth dry and her breathing painfully short by the time she had manoeuvred her way across the width of the room. Her goal was in sight—mere steps away—when a penetrating voice braked her speeding feet.

'Elise Portland! Heavens, I hardly knew you!' When a detaining hand fastened upon her arm Elise faltered, experiencing dread.

'Hello, Janine,' she replied weakly, intuitively sensing the presence of the girl's sister.

A figure detached itself from a nearby group, blonde, willowy, her face alive with anticipation. 'Elise, how devastating you look!' Camilla purred, eyes cat-bright. 'At last I've discovered someone who might be able to tell me of Jacques' whereabouts! It's six hours since we landed on the island, yet not one person I've spoken to has been able to give me the information I require. Where is he, do you know?'

Pinned by two pairs of inquisitive eyes, Elise could do no more than stammer, 'He ... he's about somewhere——'

'You mean he's actually here at the Sirocco?' Camilla pressed, a flow of pink beautifying her petal-textured skin. Elise capitulated. No one could expect to challenge Camilla's appeal and hope to win. Not only was she exceptionally beautiful, she oozed self-confidence, so assured that whatever she wanted she would get that everyone else merely had to bow to the inevitable.

'Yes, he's here, but we were just about to leave,' she admitted, biting a wayward bottom lip. 'He's gone to fetch my wrap.'

If a whip had cracked Camilla could not have

looked more startled. The minutes used in greeting had not been wasted; even while pleasantries were being exchanged her quick eyes had noted the new maturity blooming over childish features. The girl is over-made-up and under-dressed, she decided with contempt, hearing warning bells ringing in the background of her mind; her attempted sophistication is an obvious ploy to win Jacques' attention.

Feeling a stir of anger, she examined the avant-garde dress exposing unripened beauty previously left unscarred by lascivious stares. Lips trembling under a weight of violent colour were a caricature of voluptuous infancy and blackened eyelashes and tinted lids were drooping over eyes that were frankly scared! Camilla's lips tightened. Ordinarily, she was too well aware of her own attractions to allow opposition to worry her, but Jacques was unpredictable, so impulsive he could well be led astray. Her knowledge of him brought sudden fear —chivalrous, protective, unthinking, careless—he could be all of these. How had he reacted to this contradictory, seductive cherub?

The light laugh she managed brilliantly covered up her surging animosity. 'How thoughtful of Jacques to entertain you while I was away. However, now that I'm back, I'm afraid you must resign yourself to seeing less of him for a while. We have lots to talk over and he must begin to get further acquainted with my father and with my young sister Janine, who'll be staying with us permanently now that she's finished school. By the way,' she looked puzzled, 'how did you two happen to be-

'come acquainted? I didn't know you were friends.'

'We attended the same school,' Janine chipped in, tearing envious eyes away from Elise, whose appearance epitomized all she herself hoped to achieve.

'Then why didn't you say so earlier?' Camilla snapped. 'The mention of Jamaica must have brought her name to mind.'

'Why should it?' Janine replied, intent upon examining the intricate embroidery. 'I knew Elise lived here, of course, but I imagined she'd reside in Paris or somewhere equally exciting once she married the Comte de Montague.'

'*Elise* marry the Comte de Montague?' Camilla echoed on a peal of laughter. 'Silly child, it's I who is to marry the Comte! Don't you *ever* listen, Janine?'

Her derogatory tone sparked an indignant reply from her sister. 'Of course I do! You mentioned your friend Jacques, and how much you adore him, but if you'd thought to mention that his title is the Comte de Montague I could have told you then that he and Elise planned to be married as soon as she finished school. It was arranged years ago when they were children,' she faltered, dismayed by her sister's expression of shocked disbelief.

No one in the surrounding crowd suspected that the three girls chatting together were enmeshed within a triangle of drama. Nor did they notice the man making his way towards them who stopped at the sound of Janine's penetrating voice.

Miserably, Elise faced Camilla's accusing stare. '*You* expect to become Jacques' bride?' she derided, forgetting for once to modulate her tone. Elise examined her sandals, concerning herself as one so often does in moments of tension with the trivial fact that she had forgotten to paint her toenails. But even as she hesitated, squirming under Camilla's compelling stare, she knew the moment of truth was upon her. Without lifting her head she nodded, then, just as she was about to begin an explanation, Jacques' voice broke smoothly into the silence. '*Expect* is a term no longer appropriate. Elise and I were married this morning.'

Three heads lifted simultaneously and with an enigmatic smile he surveyed faces registering varying degrees of surprise. To Janine he sketched a salute, assuring her: 'You are almost as lovely as your sister,' thereby adding yet one more scalp to his belt.

Camilla remained very still, her proud eyes glittering with an emotion almost akin to hate. 'I hope you had a pleasant trip?' he enquired with a coolness that fired rather than quenched. For seconds they fenced, their eyes locked in silent conflict, then just when Elise felt she could no longer endure the atmosphere of ragged emotion Camilla dispersed tension with a haughty toss of her head.

'Congratulations to you both,' she offered with admirable control. 'Tomorrow I must see about buying you a wedding present.'

Elise almost shied away when his hand descended upon her shoulder, but his grip tightened as negligently he replied, 'We would prefer that you and your friends join us in a celebration, wouldn't we, *ma petite*?' he urged Elise, his hand increasing its pressure on her flimsily-covered shoulder.

'Yes, indeed . . .' prodded by pain, she gasped out the lie, 'that would be delightful.'

During the following hours she experienced the confusing joy of being the recipient of Jacques' complete attention. He deferred to her every wish, consulting with her before ordering to ensure that each course was to her liking, deriding a little her taste in wine but coaxing her to sample his own by pouring minute quantities into her glass and smiling tenderly when the very dry vintage assaulted her untried palate, causing her to cough.

The management were swift to accommodate the enlarged party; two adjoining tables were pushed together in a secluded alcove and as the evening progressed more and more glances were directed towards the party whose escalating merriment cast doubts upon rumours of discord between the handsome Comte and the girl who had been his constant companion weeks before his surprising marriage.

Jeremy Sherlock arrived too late to be warned that the quiet dinner party he had been anticipating had turned into a wedding celebration, and the cynicism of his glance when he was introduced to the young bride caused her a slipped heartbeat. Jacques, however, seemed not to notice that his congratulations held grave reserve.

'But why the need for secrecy?' Camilla probed with pretended gaiety once Jeremy had been seated. 'Surely your friends were entitled to be present at the ceremony? Even if you scorn support, their good wishes would hardly have come amiss!'

'We neither of us felt in need of support,' Jacques

returned, raising Elise's fingers to his lips to kiss each tip one by one. 'Besides, a large reception would not have seemed proper so soon after the death of Elise's grandmother!'

'I'm sorry, Elise, I had no idea!' Camilla's quick apology was accompanied by a start of surprise. After a second's thought, she rallied. 'Your grandmother was your only living relative, I believe? Her death must have left you totally unsupported—even the house she lived in belonged to the estate of Montague.' She paused, her glance swivelling towards Jacques, then swiftly back to Elise with, for the first time that evening, a glimmer of triumph in her eyes. 'Jacques, despite his deliberately assumed attitude of disinterest in other people's affairs, is given to chivalrous impulses, as no doubt you're aware, Elise. How fortunate for you that he was at hand when you needed a shoulder to cry on—I imagine your tears would react upon his sympathies like acid upon armour.'

Silken stress was placed upon the words which sounded to everyone pleasantly congratulatory. But within full range of her assault Elise was aware that Camilla's suspicions were aroused. A cold shiver feathered her warm skin. Camilla wanted Jacques more than she had ever wanted anything or anyone—which boded ill for the one already in possession!

'Shall we dance, Elise?' Jacques' query was a lifeline seized eagerly.

'Yes, please . . .' She almost stumbled in her haste to leave the radius of Camilla's assessment, feeling relief only when they reached the dance floor and she was enfolded into Jacques' powerful arms.

'You're trembling!' he accused, pulling her closer so that her head was resting against his broad chest. The beat of his heart was reassuring, projecting strength, power and security. His reaction to Camilla's appearance indicated that he was determined to hide their secret from outsiders—not even the attraction she held for him was to be allowed to invalidate the marriage vows he had made just a few hours ago. But he had also promised punishment, and not even with the devil's help could he have devised a more painful torture than that of adopting the role of lover when all he really felt was hate.

His lips branded her brow, arousing contradictory feelings of ecstasy and despair. 'Must you do that?' she protested weakly.

He smiled and continued guiding her around the dance floor, then before an interested audience he lowered his head to brush his lips along the curve of her cheek, lingering long enough to mutter, 'I'd rather Camilla thought me fickle than a fool! She must be convinced that we're in love, I refuse to allow her the amusement of finding out how easily I was tricked into marriage by a conniving child!'

'You *asked* me to marry you!' she hissed back.

'And you accepted, knowing what I did not!' he gritted, hiding his fury behind a deceiving smile.

As they circled the dance floor—lovers swaying to the music of seductive strings—the thrust of words continued.

'I did you a favour!' she protested. 'You are not, and never were in love with Camilla—you simply felt piqued because you thought you'd been ditched!'

He winced. 'Spare me the juvenile expressions, and please try to remember your position, even if it's beyond your capabilities to live up to it!'

As usual, his was the last word. Elise lapsed into silence, seething behind a mask of calm, and for the rest of the evening refused to be drawn into further clashes with the man whose split role of lover and enemy was reacting upon her nerves like refined torture.

He danced once with Camilla, devouring her beautiful face but handling her gently, much as a connoisseur would handle a fragile piece of china. Elise could not bear to look, so she tore troubled eyes away from the engrossed couple, only to blunder straight into the sights of Jeremy Sherlock, whose look dissected with the precision of a surgeon's knife.

'Poor Elise,' he murmured without sympathy.

Resenting his insight into her innermost thoughts, she replied with hauteur, '*Poor* is a word hardly applicable to the wife of a wealthy *comte*, Doctor Sherlock.'

He shrugged. 'I refer not to what you have but to what you crave, Comtesse,' his smile was uncomfortably knowing. 'Great desire is allied to great fear, as I think you're already beginning to find out.'

'I've never been good at guessing riddles,' she reached nervously for her wine glass. 'And I will never understand you—a man content to keep his love hidden. Why don't you try to make her jealous, doctor?' she goaded with spirit. 'Camilla has no interest in what's readily available, so why not forsake your English inhibitions and accept that it's as healthy to enjoy love as it is to enjoy strawberry jam!'

Her contempt stung. Dull colour rose under his tan and his aloof expression gave way to anger. 'Why, you ...!' he began, then checked himself when he realized Camilla and Jacques were advancing towards the table. Both became suddenly aware of their close proximity and they edged apart, feeling like conspirators. Elise suffered a keenly suspicious glance from her husband and Camilla looked startled—Jeremy's devotion, although undemonstrated, had always cushioned her background; the look she gave Elise showed resentment of the intimacy implied by deep conversation and closely held heads. Dislike sparked between the two men before, with arrogant disregard of the wishes of the rest of the party, Jacques slicked back his cuff to examine his watch. 'Time to go,' he indicated to Elise, 'we have a long drive back across the island.'

Only minutes after edging the monster Citroën from out of its parking spot he began an inquisition into the length and depth of her association with Jeremy.

'I know him only as Grand'mère's doctor!' she protested, put on the defensive by his arbitrary questions. 'Usually he seems to find it difficult even to be civil!'

'A man in love adopts many strange attitudes,' he shot. 'Shyness often hides behind a façade of reserve and even abruptness can have its roots in frustration. Women delight in teasing men whose adoration is made obvious, but conversely they're always ready to tempt a man to respond to encouragement.'

'Encouragement? You're surely not implying that the doctor and I were enjoying a flirtation? Why, Jeremy is so much in love with Camilla he even tried to discourage my relationship with you in order to spare her pain!'

'I find that difficult to believe in the light of his behaviour this evening,' he countered with all the resentment of an outraged husband. 'Camilla was available, yet at the first opportunity he turned his attention upon you! Think again about the motivation behind his attempt to interfere with our relationship—it seems more than likely that his concern was not for Camilla but for yourself!'

His accusation had the effect of a shower of cold water—breathtaking at first but with an aftermath of exhilaration. Jacques, fanatically opposed to the relinquishing of anything that was his, was showing all the symptoms of jealousy! Of course he would deny it if challenged, would laugh to scorn any suggestion that he could consider her of any worth, but whether he liked it or not the years of childish confidences, the hours of happy companionship, had forged fragile links which were reacting upon his subconscious with the resilience of steel!

She stepped from the car glowing like a bride and found his glowering features not in the least disconcerting as he escorted her into the Grand House, then followed her into the salon where he poured amber wine into tall stemmed glasses and helped her to tiny sandwiches left under a covered salver by the ever-thoughtful Mattie. With a smile ghosting her lips Elise munched away, ignoring his restless prowling and the interrogative glances cast from eyes dangerous as racing seas.

It could have been her smile, or perhaps it was her cool indifference to his displeasure that caused him to act, but suddenly she was lifted from her chair and planted squarely on her feet.

'Time you went to bed,' he dismissed curtly, directing her towards the door.

With quick insight she noted signs of unease and was made femininely aware of her own desirability by the reluctant way his glance slid over curves thrusting provocatively through the material as insubstantial as golden mist. Some devil of flirtation urged her to test out her newly sensed power. 'Will you come up soon ...?' she breathed shyly.

An audible rasp was her only answer. Towering still and tall, he returned her look of tender yearning with one of blank control.

Daring all on one fateful chance, she drifted closer and slid tentative arms along stiffened shoulders, willing him to respond to her consuming need. It was rapture to feel his arms tighten around her waist, to feel her weakness propped up by his strength. Desire escalated as his hands held her firm, making no effort to exploit her rising passion. Rendered wanton, she pressed hungry lips against his stern mouth, and felt rebuffed when her fire was met with ice and the sharp edge of her ecstasy was blunted against his granite control. Not a muscle of his body reacted when with a small defeated moan she collapsed against him—a slender stem starved of love.

'Go to bed.' His voice sounded disembodied, way above her head.

His composure insulted her quivering nerves, heaped scorn upon the immature advances she had employed to arouse him. Feeling wretchedly humiliated, she withdrew from arms extended only as support. As she did so, a brown wing of hair fell across her forehead and as she lifted a dispirited hand to brush it aside she glanced up and glimpsed in that split second a shadow of despair winging across his dark features. It gave her courage to appeal, 'I wanted so much to please you, Jacques. This evening I tried really hard to act as I thought you would wish me to act. I hoped . . .' her voice trembled, but after a deep-breath she forced out the confession, 'I hoped that if I should succeed you might begin to regard me as a woman—as a wife—but if that's too much to hope for,' lashes swept down to hide shame as she offered in a choked whisper '. . . I'll be content to take the place of a mistress.'

His answer was swift, raw with frustration. 'That, too, was my hope, but I find it's no longer possible. I can't make love to you when with every look I'm reminded of slippers with bunny motifs, Mickey Mouse tee-shirts and a childish face smeared with jam! Our marriage was a great mistake,' he stated bitterly. 'Ahead of us lie years of misery, but you must look to me for neither sympathy nor help, because whatever the extent of our wretchedness you must acknowledge equal blame!'

94

CHAPTER EIGHT

It was hard to adjust to the idea of Jeremy Sherlock as an ally, but during the long, lonely weeks following, when Jacques left her to her own devices. Elise found a measure of relief in combating Jeremy's somewhat abrasive lectures on the futility of giving way to self-pity.

'Why can't you go away and leave me alone!' she snapped when his shadow loomed yet again, obscuring the sun's rays from her bikini-clad body.

'I keep asking myself that,' he replied, ignoring her irritable shrug and stretching out next to her on the beach.

'And might I ask what answer you get?' she asked sarcastically, wanting only to be left to wallow in the misery of her empty marriage.

'I tell myself that a doctor must study the state of his patient's mental as well as her physical health. I know that ... business is keeping Jacques occupied in Kingston, and that you seldom have any company other than that of servants, therefore I reckon it is my clear duty to infiltrate your solitude in order to ensure you don't end up talking a load of gibberish to people who aren't even there.'

She jerked her toast-brown body upright and glared. 'For one thing,' she spat, 'I'm not your patient! And for another, I'm perfectly well aware that you only come to gloat, to turn the screw by reminding me that you were right!'

Steadily, he returned her tempestuous look, his sympathetic expression giving rise to further rage. 'Have I ever said I told you so?' he enquired mildly.

Her young limbs, scantily clad in scraps of brilliant cotton, remained tense for a second, then after a reluctant shake of her head she slumped back on to the sand. 'Not yet, you haven't,' she acceded grudgingly, 'but I can sense your urge to do so every time we meet.'

He laughed, admiring her frankness. 'Then you sense wrongly. I must admit to an ulterior motive, but it's one you can hardly censure, seeing the idea was originally yours.'

'Mine?' Her interest was caught.

'Didn't you urge me to make Camilla jealous? After due deliberation I decided you might possibly be right, so, knowing that you, being aware of the situation, could never misconstrue my actions, I concluded that my ideal partner would be you.'

For the first time in weeks Elise felt like laughing. 'Me? You think Camilla could become jealous of *me*? Oh, doctor,' she gurgled, 'might I suggest you visit an optician!'

He bent across, his glance hardening. 'There's nothing wrong with my eyesight, it's your ridiculous lack of confidence that's at fault—due, I've no doubt to the hammering it's taken from your blinkered husband who's too obsessed with what he thinks he wants to appreciate what he already has. But even he will be having to rethink, I shouldn't wonder.' He surprised her with a lighthearted grin. 'Do you know that since your appearance at the Sirocco the whole of Kingston has been raving

From Harlequin...a special offer for women who enjoy reading fascinating stories of great romance in exciting places...

ACCEPT THIS "COLLECTOR'S EDITION" FREE...

...JUST FOR TELLING US WHY YOU LIKE TO READ ROMANTIC FICTION!

Please take a minute to fill out the attached questionnaire... affix your "YES" stamp... and mail today! We pay postage.

Harlequin's Collection 1

.75
72006

VIOLET WINSPEAR
Lucifer's Angel

Keep your free copy of this special "Collector's Edition"...

Please answer the simple questions on the card, detach and mail today. We'll be happy to send you this special "Collector's Edition" of *Lucifer's Angel* by Violet Winspear absolutely free. It's our way of saying "Thank you" for helping us publish more of the kind of books you like to read.

One of the classic romance novels by this world-renowned author! You'll enjoy reading Violet Winspear's explosive story of the fast-moving hard-living world of Hollywood in the '50s. It's an unforgettable tale of an innocent young girl who meets and marries a dynamic but ruthless movie producer. It's a gripping novel combining excitement, intrigue, mystery and romance.

Newly printed in a special "Collector's Edition"! We've published a brand new "Collector's Edition" of Violet Winspear's first Harlequin novel. And a complimentary copy is waiting for you. Just fill out the card and mail today.

about the Comte's ravishingly attractive bride? He must be having quite a job to explain your absence, even though most evenings he has a creditable substitute by his side,' he concluded with a wry grimace.

'Camilla!' she stated flatly, needing no confirmation. Only one person could be claiming so much of Jacques' time. Each morning after breakfast he left the house whistling and did not return until the early hours of next day, still whistling and with such a spring in his step that the ancient banisters rattled as he bounded up the stairs. She swallowed painfully, paying strict attention to a flag of sail just visible on the horizon. 'Why have you changed your mind about Jacques and Camilla? Only weeks ago you challenged me to separate them, even dared me to believe that they could ever find happiness apart, yet now ...'

'*Now*, the Comte is married,' he cut in. 'Because of his deep-rooted sense of family honour, he will never contemplate divorce. Gossip he'll shrug off, but I don't intend to stand by while Camilla is made unhappy, as she surely will be once she discovers that she can never mean any more to him than a passing affair. She will find that shattering,' he rapped, frustrated by his own helplessness. 'That's why I'm willing to try anything that might help put an end to this attachment before it goes too far. But even if my plan doesn't succeed,' worried fingers raked through a thatch of blond hair, 'at least I'll be sufficiently informed to know when to be ready to pick up the pieces.'

The sun grew hot on their bodies as they lay

bathing in its warmth, Jeremy brooding upon the girl who took his adoration so much for granted, and Elise silently assessing the danger of arousing the black anger of a man whose slave-trading ancestors had shown no mercy to defaulters of either sex. Like Caesar, he demanded a wife beyond reproach, at least in the eyes of others. To pay him back in his own coin would require the utmost courage, especially when it meant subjecting him to the ridicule of his friends. Had she the strength to inflict such a thrashing upon his pride?

Jeremy did not press her for a decision, but waited patiently, knowing the love she felt for her husband was great enough to prod her into accepting any chance to end the deadlock strangling their marriage. Nevertheless, he was relieved to hear her oblique acceptance.

'It's just as well I'm not one of your patients,' she strove to sound flippant, 'otherwise the threat of professional misconduct might have overshadowed our proposed entanglement.'

With quick ease he stood up, pulling her to her feet. 'Can I take it that you're agreeable?' he quizzed. She inhaled deeply, then nodded. 'Good, then we must plan our offensive carefully. Tonight a floor show is due to open at the Roof Garden, and all of Kingston's notables will be there—including us!'

Elise remained thinking long after Jeremy—who had instructed her to be ready when he returned later that evening—had left to resume his round. She was not regretting her decision; any form of action was preferable to continuing the monotonous routine she had been forced to endure because of Jacques' flagrant neglect. At first, she had tried with enthusiasm to make the vast interior of the Grand House more homely. She had begun by gathering masses of flowers from the garden and arranging them in urns and vases which she placed at strategic points around the house, concentrating upon the main hall where Jacques could not fail to see them when either entering or leaving. She had found the cavernous fireplace an ideal spot for an arrangement of flowering shrubs—poinciana, with its feathery leaves and flame-coloured flowers; yellow, bell-shaped allamanda blossoms, bougainvillea, hibiscus, oleander and poinsettia—she experimented with them all, patiently replacing the short-lived plants each morning, hoping her efforts were being appreciated by the man whose desire for comfort had led to the labour of love. But when he had returned home one night and blundered into a display barely visible in the gloom of the hall his swift imprecation had been audible enough to reach her bedroom. With cheeks the colour of the flaming poinciana he had sent crashing to the floor she had decided that her efforts were being regarded more of a nuisance than an improvement and had immediately abandoned the chore.

One of her successes, however, had been the furnishing of a small room she had discovered stacked with rubbish on the ground floor. A request to Mattie had resulted in its being entirely cleared, revealing a room, minute by Grand House standards, flooded from floor to ceiling with golden sunshine.

'Wonderful!' Elise had congratulated the beaming Mattie. 'At last I'll have somewhere where I can relax in comfort, a room I can make my very own. And look!' she flung open French windows and stepped outside into a part of the garden that had been allowed to become overgrown. 'If we can find some garden furniture, a table, a couple of chairs—perhaps even a hammock—I'll even have my own secret garden!'

'Lawdie, Missis Elise, ain't you got no place t' sit?' Mattie questioned wide-eyed, unable in her simplicity to understand the need for sanctuary in the midst of plenty.

'No place where I feel at home,' she supplied gravely. 'All the rooms in this house have been furnished for women of aristocratic tastes by men eager to please. My tastes are simple, but even when I've finished with this room I doubt if Jacques will see it, he's too uninterested to care ...'

She had seen the perplexity on Mattie's face and realized, too late, how unwisely her tongue had been allowed to ramble. Summoning a smile, she had urged brightly, 'Let's get cracking, shall we? My mind is teeming with ideas I can hardly wait to put into practice.' Mattie had responded with a slow deliberation that had betrayed a problem on her mind and Elise had been able to do no more than bite her lip, hoping time would erase from Mattie's memory the heartbreak contained in her unthinking outburst.

She was tired by the time she dragged herself up from the beach and entered the massive hall, its walls hung with flags and burnished breastplates decorated with crosses, fleurs-de-lis and other insignia discarded by the long-dead Montagues staring fixedly from out of gilt-framed canvases ranged along an upper gallery. She shivered, knowing the glances would have been equally derogatory had their owners been alive. Did they somehow know, she wondered as she hurried towards her den, about the tricks she was planning to play upon their unsuspecting descendant? She stifled a scream when a sound like the striking of a massive gong startled her. Someone, somewhere in the house, had dropped a hollow metal object—one of the huge brass preserving pans, perhaps, she consoled herself as the noise bounced from feet-thick walls to pluck an hysterical tune of threat from her nerve-strings. With the echo still lingering in the background, she gasped and ran, seeking escape from the vengeance-bent spirits she felt sure were pressing on her heels.

She was breathless by the time she reached her room, but from the moment she entered peace calmed her over-wrought nerves. The furnishings were a hotch-potch of pieces sorted from attics crammed with long-discarded articles. No single item was of outstanding significance, yet each corner held some pleasant visual surprise. Still wearing her beach robe, she wandered across to admire once again a fruitwood stand inset with Delft tiles which she had utilized as a jardinière. A riot of pink and red geraniums were reflected in a thoughtfully-placed mirror which also had caught on its surface a glimpse of carefully arranged still-lifes on an opposite wall. Floral print curtains billowed in a breeze from the open window and matching material covered the comfortably upholstered wood and cane settee. Elise threw herself down upon the settee, kicked off her rubber flip-flops and ran her toes through the curled fleece of a sheepskin rug. She smiled, loving the comfort of soft wool underfoot, and relaxed with a sigh of contentment, bathed in cool light filtering through closed shutters.

Much later Jacques' voice called her by name. She jerked upright from her coiled position, wondering, as she fought the languorous aftermath of deep sleep, if the voice were real or a figment of her imagination. But when she heard him calling for Mattie in an irritable vein she knew that Jacques had indeed arrived—a most unusual occurrence so early in the day!

Luxuriously she stretched, not in the least inclined to hasten to do his bidding, feeling safe in the room which so far as he knew did not exist. An enjoyable yawn was cut short when after an interchange with Mattie his footsteps began approaching down the passageway. *Mattie, you fool!* she muttered, realizing that the secret of her hideout had been disclosed. She sprang up to escape into the garden, but the shutter handles were stiff with disuse and resisted all pressure from her hand. She was standing like an animal at bay when the door crashed open, revealing Jacques glowering on the threshold.

'*Sacre-bleu!*' His black eyebrows elevated. 'What have you done to the cloakroom?'

'Oh, is that what it is—was?' she amended brightly, shifting nervously back to the settee. 'I've made it into a den—a private den,' she emphasized, peeping under downswept lashes to gauge the effect of her claim.

As he strode inside muscles rippled under a chest-hugging shirt open at the neck to display a gold medallion swinging against his throat. Tensely, Elise watched as he walked towards a chair, his lithe movements made pantherish by slacks tailored to his hips like a second skin. He looked around, taking so long she felt sure her work was being appreciated, but the small smile disappeared from her lips when he congratulated, 'You've done very well, I feel I can relax quite easily in here!'

'You will not!' she defended, fiercely resenting the implied take-over. 'I did all the work, so I'm entitled to keep the room entirely to myself. You already have a study, a library, half a dozen salons, so why do you need to make territorial demands upon a room you'd forgotten ever existed until a few minutes ago?'

'Territorial demands?' he repeated blandly. 'Such an expression is meaningless between husband and wife. What I own is yours, just as whatever is yours you will share with me. Yes!' he settled into his chair, resting his head upon the comfortable back, 'you have done well, *chérie*, I feel we will share many relaxing hours in this nest you have created.'

We! The assumption of possession stung her into unwise retaliation. Annoyed as a bee ousted from its hive, she hovered above him, buzzing angrily. 'Like your ancestors, you're not content to possess —you must seize and plunder and——'

'Rape?' he suggested helpfully when further words failed her. Elise spun on her heel, not daring to face the glint of piracy her accusation had aroused. He was in a teasing, good-tempered mood, brought on, no doubt, by the attractive, congenial companion he had recently left. The thought spurred her on to an even rasher outburst.

'How much does possession rule your desire for Camilla, I wonder? Your vanity was crippled by her supposed rejection, do you seek to heal it by acquiring what you thought was lost?'

She gave a shocked start when he loomed up behind her to clip, 'Charm is not inherent in ownership, Madame la Comtesse. For instance, I find no pleasure in the possession of a jealous-tongued wife who schemed and planned to break up an attachment merely to gain security for herself!'

She faced him, proud and deeply hurt. 'If that's the excuse you've seized upon to condone your behaviour I won't even bother to refute it. We both know that what you've just said is untrue—I've never had any desire for material things, neither did I scheme or plan. Though I knew you were attracted to Camilla, I never believed you two were suited.'

Her small, earnest face pleaded for his understanding, but he had been too well aggravated. As always, whenever they made contact, her opposition struck sparks from his flint. 'How can you deny duplicity when before an assembled company you admitted telling Janine that a marriage had been arranged between us when we were children and that as soon as your schooling was finished you were

104

immediately to become my bride? Camilla is an angel not to have shunned me for ever after hearing such a lie!'

'It was no lie—I did believe . . .' With heightened colour Elise stammered out the reminder. 'You asked me to marry you just before you left the island, don't you remember? We spent your last day at the Cove of Promises and before we parted you said that when you returned you would make me your wife. I still have the ring you gave me,' she rushed on eagerly, encouraged by his look of stunned recollection. 'It's upstairs in my room, I'll go and fetch it!'

When Jacques detained her by grasping her elbow she swung round with eyes shining, but the glow dimmed when with an incredulous inflection he condemned:

'You surely didn't take seriously the ramblings of an adolescent whose only contact with the female sex was with a child and her grandmother? Don't think me ungrateful!' he protested swiftly. 'I owe a great deal to your grandmother and probably . . .' he hesitated as if faced with an unpalatable truth, 'to you. I suppose I loved you both, in a way,' he admitted slowly, 'certainly I regarded Madame Calvet as a mother and you . . .' he searched her expressive face and found sweetness and devotion written in brown velvet eyes and an unknowingly quivering mouth. 'I suppose I must have loved you as a sister,' he insisted grimly, deflating all hope. He shook his head as if to clear his mind of spectres from the past before impressing slowly, 'No sane person could expect me to honour promises made in callow youth, or to benefit in any way from such promises.'

Elise weathered the blow even though her heart cried out to remind him that although she had been very much younger *her* love had stood the test of time. 'There was never any question of my benefiting,' she replied with dignity, 'just of being faithful.'

'You were only nine years old!' he protested savagely.

'But a thousand years wise, I think,' she sighed.

She was aghast to see how uncomfortable she had made him with her protestations of a love he had neither wanted nor sought. Quickly, she reassured him: 'I'm sorry if I've embarrassed you, I realize now that you don't owe me a thing! It's curious,' she exclaimed with sudden insight, 'but discussing the subject seems to have put an entirely new slant on our relationship. I can see now how stupidly foolish I've been—all these years my mind has been occupied only with thoughts of you, leaving me no time to think of anyone else!' As she began studying him with a mixture of wonder and curiosity his nostrils took on a haughty flare. 'I've been a fool!' she decided, placing unflattering emphasis. 'In future you'll have no reason to complain further about my childish behaviour. It's unfortunate that the mistake we made in marrying can't be rectified in a hurry, but it shouldn't be impossible for each of us to salvage something out of the situation.'

Jacques looked arrogantly taken aback at the idea of his having to consider her well-being, but was relieved enough to agree. 'Of course you will find compensations,' he waved a vague hand, 'there's your room, and the garden, and your duties as hostess, certainly it shouldn't be impossible for us to achieve an atmosphere of harmony.'

Provided he was left free to pursue his own pleasures, she was shrewd enough to conclude. Suspicion lurked in his eyes as he studied her innocent expression, but then he shrugged, feeling confident of his ability to ensure no action of hers would be allowed to alter the tenor of his ways.

'We must agree to compromise,' he told her, looking slightly bored.

'We must,' she agreed, then with a dash of cynicism, 'Who knows, our artificial marriage may turn out to be just as good as the real!'

CHAPTER NINE

IT was with a light heart that Elise began dressing for her evening out with Jeremy. Her declaration of independence had not been entirely motivated by bravado; in some miraculous way she felt she had been relieved of a burden. For years Jacques had been the cog around which her every thought and action had revolved, schooldays had been an abyss through which she had had to pass before achieving ultimate happiness; the boring ritual of learning social graces had been weathered merely so that she would not disgrace the position she had thought to occupy and also, because she had thought her future so well defined, even the youthful pastime of falling in and out of love had been denied her.

However, once Jacques had scoured her mind of the last traces of childhood fantasy she was able to judge the situation from his position—but cringed from the picture that developed. Regarded in the cold light of reason, the idea of having expected him to honour his boyhood proposal was laughable—but perversely she wept for the part she had played in bringing about their marriage. But then with youthful optimism she decided no irretrievable harm had been done; annulment did not carry the same stigma as divorce and so for Jacques' sake, in an attempt to atone for the wrong she had done him, she intended suggesting this to him as a method of resolving their dilemma.

She hummed to herself as she stepped into her dress and twirled before a full-length mirror satisfied that the white sunray-embroidered sari with pearl-trimmed hem contrasted nicely against her tan. She frowned, feeling guiltily aware as she peeped across her shoulder that Jacques would not approve of the amount of flesh left exposed by the length of material fashioned into a dress that had neither buttons nor fasteners to secure its folds, crossed halter-wise around her neck, with ends tied loosely; her shoulders, arms and back were bare, inviting stares of admiration as well as speculative looks from many who were bound to wonder whether the flimsy construction would stand up to the rigours of even one evening. She shrugged, then half-smiling, clipped a jewelled butterfly on to her carefully casual hairstyle and slipped dozens of wire-thin silver bracelets around her wrist, enjoying the musical jangle that accompanied every movement of her arm. Conscious of escalating excitement, she grabbed a wrap and ran downstairs. Enough of her life had been wasted mooning over a man who did not want her, for twenty years she had merely existed, now was the time to begin to live!

The roof garden was packed with first-nighters, but their table had been booked weeks beforehand by a patient who, because of a sudden indisposition, had insisted upon Jeremy taking up the reservation. It was well placed near the edge of the dance floor where the cabaret was to take place, and as they edged their way forward a hush fell upon the crowd and heads swivelled to a table nearby where another party was in the process of being seated.

'Good timing, don't you think?' Jeremy murmured. 'Jacques and Camilla, together with friends, have just arrived.'

Elise craned forward, feeling happy and relaxed in Jeremy's undemanding company. Jacques' dark head was towering above the crowd and as he turned in their direction she waved gaily. 'Has he seen us, do you think?' she questioned Jeremy, slightly disappointed that her wave had not been returned.

'I believe he has—just,' Jeremy encouraged with a smile. 'Out of the corner of my eye I think I see him approaching, so don't flag, remember a lot will hang or fall on our ability as actors!'

The reminder came as a shock, so much had happened since the idea was first mooted. She no longer wished to make Jacques jealous, nor did she now believe the possibility had ever existed. But she had nothing to lose by helping Jeremy, she decided, shrugging off a sense of disloyalty to Jacques with the reminder that should Camilla prove fickle he would be the more fortunate of the two.

Jacques was upon them almost before her thoughts were untangled. The displeasure cut deep into his dark features was emphasized by a muscle jerking in his jaw.

'So you did see me after all!' she dimpled, ignoring his scowl. 'When you didn't return my wave I thought I'd been overlooked!'

'*C'est impossible!*' he declared, sweeping an icy glance across her bare shoulders. 'Are you blind that you cannot see yourself the cynosure of all eyes?'

'I am?' When she looked around and saw that he was right her eyes widened with surprise.

'A most flattering occurrence for any escort!' Jeremy's observation did nothing to erase the black shadow from Jacques' features. 'But do sit down, old man,' Jeremy mocked, 'your rather belligerent stance seems to be creating something of a stir in our vicinity!' When a disdainful look flashed his way Jeremy parried it with a smile, nevertheless he sighed his relief when Jacques arrogantly deigned to pull up a chair.

'Have some champagne,' Elise coaxed with a smile. 'It's delicious, so bubbly and high-spirited. Champagne is the only possible choice when one wants to be gay, don't you agree?'

Jacques was obviously finding it difficult to curb his temper, but conscious that his emotions were on display he made a masterly effort to achieve composure. 'I had no idea you intended coming here this evening,' he accused, culling up a smile that failed to reach his eyes. 'I suppose you meant to tell me but it slipped your mind?'

'Would you have been interested?' Her genuine surprise sent colour racing under his tan.

'Certainly I would!' he reprimanded, his sharp eyes raking a warning across Jeremy's bland features. 'If you are not careful in your choice of words, *chérie, monsieur le docteur* may form the impression that I am a neglectful husband—he might even decide that the consoling of bored young brides comes within his professional province,' he rasped. 'But then,' he relented with a softness more deadly than anger, 'a man would have to be a fool to make such an error of judgement and whatever your motive may be, *docteur*, I'm sure it is one that has been well thought out!'

Jeremy's amusement was a masterpiece of acting. 'Come now, *monsieur*, this is the twentieth century when wives demand to be treated as equals, not confined to purdah within their own homes or treated like sinners if they so much as look at another man! You're surely not suggesting that because I asked Elise to dine with me she'll become prey to other less savoury suggestions? I've formed an impression that you're both very modern in your approach to marriage and I commend such thinking. Indeed, I can imagine nothing more stupid than having to sever all friendships with the opposite sex simply because of marriage, and by your own actions, *monsieur*, you've shown that in this respect, at least, we are in entire agreement!'

'How astute of you, Jeremy!' Elise eyed him with respect. 'Jacques and I were discussing that very subject only this afternoon when we both decided that to follow a civilized code of conduct which allows equal freedom to both partners is infinitely preferable to married bondage. We agreed, didn't we, Jacques, to follow our own independent impulses rather than be bound by the tradition of being always together, always in the same place at the same time. What was the phrase you used ...? Oh, yes, I remember now,' her beam was returned by a stare, '*to achieve an atmosphere of harmony!* Don't you think,' she appealed to Jeremy, 'that that was very well put?'

'Very,' Jeremy agreed dryly, shrewdly judging

Jacques' reaction to this summing up of rules designed solely to benefit himself as one of outrage. Elise smiled upon them both, happy to have resolved a situation which at one time had seemed fraught with danger. She could not understand Jacques' attitude, nor why he was eyeing Jeremy with a restrained savagery all the more violent because it was mute.

'Don't let us keep you from your friends, *monsieur*,' Jeremy pushed his luck. 'I suspect, from their concerned looks, that they're anxious that you should join them before the show begins.'

Jacques' look pierced. No one ordered, nor even mildly directed, the Comte de Montague when his mood was less than mellow. 'I have a better plan,' he almost kicked away his chair. 'I insist you both join my party. Come, Elise,' he tugged her to her feet, 'Camilla and Janine will be disappointed if you refuse.'

'Chance would be a fine thing!' she muttered under her breath, resenting his bulldozing methods. But protest would have been useless—like a stampeding stallion, he would trample anything placed in his path! As graciously as she could manage she allowed him to escort her across to the table where a fuming Camilla and an assortment of interested friends had to be rearranged to accommodate the additions to their party. Mercifully, the lights dimmed the instant they were seated and trying social backchat was rendered unnecessary by the opening of the show.

Somehow, in the confusion, Jeremy and she had been separated and when she twisted round in the darkness to commend an artiste to her nearest companion it was Jacques' voice that reached her through thundering applause. His austere reply dampened her enjoyment and during the rest of the cabaret she squirmed under his dark surveillance. Jeremy, at least, was happy, she noted with satisfaction, each time she sought him out Camilla seemed to be showering him with attention.

Once the show was over dancing was resumed and Jeremy was quick to claim her. 'Don't you want to dance with Camilla?' she questioned as they circled the floor.

'Yes,' he replied honestly, 'but the success of our gamble has so elated me I feel prepared to gamble further.'

'You mean she's jealous?' When he nodded she laughed aloud with pleased excitement and he hugged her close to whisper in her ear, 'Mademoiselle Camilla is furious—her old faithful, her dependable swain, has seen fit to switch his attentions to another. And *what* another!' he exclaimed appreciatively, captivated by the happy amber gleam in her brown velvet eyes. 'Has Jacques ever told you what a stunner you are?' he murmured, intoxicated by success and by the admiring glances being directed towards his partner.

Her silvery peal of laughter turned every head. 'Goodness, no!' she spluttered, then confided, 'Once he told me to go away and play, and another time he scolded me for having jam on my face!' When they both erupted into laughter everyone around them smiled, infected by their obvious happiness. Even the band was not immune and showed their affinity with the happy pair by continuing to play tune after tune without a pause, so helping them to retain their isolation in the midst of a crowd.

For the first time in her life Elise flirted and in return enjoyed the flattery of a young, attractive male. It was a heady experience, even headier than the champagne she had been enjoying non-stop since the evening began. Youthful high spirits bubbled into life, engendering an urge to experiment, to make up for lost time by throwing herself wholeheartedly into the discovery of delights which so far had eluded her. She wanted to forget inhibitions and to enjoy whatever was offered with complete abandon.

Jeremy was an eager participant. An accomplished dancer, he led her into complicated routines that were wildly applauded by the crowd which gradually formed itself into a circle around the edge of the dance floor. Champagne could have been responsible for the confidence with which she faultlessly followed her partner through the intricacies of a quickstep; the graceful, floating movements of a waltz, the zestful Latin rhythm of a cha-cha-cha and finally into the full-blooded, voluptuous posturings of a paso doble, a dance which began by emulating the movements of an enraged bull tormented by a toreador's waving cape, and ended with Elise, portraying a triumphant toreador, planting one small foot firmly on Jeremy's chest while he lay, a panting, mortally wounded bull, stretched out on the floor.

Laughingly, they acknowledged tumultuous applause and ear-piercing catcalls before running the

115

gauntlet of a protesting audience howling for more. On the crest of an exuberant wave they approached their table, then suffered a drench of cold anger from two pairs of astonished, resentful eyes.

It was Janine who broke the frigid silence. Afire with admiration, she congratulated, 'I say, you two were absolutely super! Just think, Elise, how furious we all were at being forced to practise such dances—you especially always professed them to be as obsolete as the dodo!'

'I never imagined dancing could be such fun,' Elise admitted, grateful to pursue the subject in order to bridge the awful gap of silence. 'But all the credit must go to my partner, without his guidance my lack of skill would have become glaringly obvious.'

'Nonsense!' Jeremy relaxed into his chair, his complacent expression further goading Camilla's resentment. 'As always, my dear, you're being far too modest.'

'Surely when a person is possessed of only moderate talent to be modest is merely to be honest,' Camilla interceded, stinging as a wasp.

Jeremy smiled, enjoying her discomfiture, then deciding she had been tormented enough he relented. 'Come along, let's both exercise our moderate talents, I know how you love to dance.'

Immediately they had disappeared Jacques extended the same invitation to Elise, but with much less enthusiasm and a frown that indicated he would not be thwarted. But instead of leading her on to the dance floor, he steered her through open French windows on to a balcony deserted except for one other couple barely discernible in the shadowy distance. In an isolated corner screened by overhanging greenery, he placed a hand on her shoulder and spun her round to face him. She braced, unable to understand in what way she had angered him but conscious that a storm was about to break. It began as a light shower of scorn, but anger growled beneath the cool patter of his words.

'Clearly, you've absorbed a few of the social graces, which surprises me considering your past indiscretions, but your education is still far from complete. Did none of your tutors ever think to warn you about the folly, not to mention danger, of egging on an impressionable, obviously infatuated male?'

'I——'

'Not only were you carrying on a flagrant flirtation out there on the dance floor,' he blocked her protest with a further spate of hail, 'you made me the object of pitying looks from people who are unused to seeing such undignified conduct from one bearing an ancient and respected name!'

'There have been occasions in the past when your own conduct has raised many eyebrows!' she flashed, incensed by his criticism.

He reached out, pinning each shoulder with a vicious grip. 'I do what I like!' he decreed, casting a menacing shadow over her bent head, 'whereas you, Madame la Comtesse, must learn to do as you are bid. You practised trickery to gain security, now you must be contented with the possessions you sought! Wealth, position, servants to do your bidding, the luxury of a grand home! Everything you schemed for you have, except one thing—a husband who loves you!'

She froze with hurt as he bent forward, hypnotizing her with a glittering stare. 'Your punishment will be to yearn for the comfort of arms holding you as close as I'm holding you now,' he declared, bending her pliant young body over a steely forearm. 'To feel lips against your throat ... warm ... exploring ... eager ...' he demonstrated, taking vicious delight in her moans for mercy as she endured his sadistic torture. She clung to him as he kissed her, drawing fire and life from every throbbing nerve. Passion lain dormant flared with ecstatic relief, an inner furnace made all the more consuming because it had been so long restrained. '*Je t'aime! ... Je t'adore!*' he tormented, his sensuous lips tracing the outline of a shell pink ear, a slender arched neck, a velvet-smooth curve of shoulder.

At the sound of a sob he lifted his head and through the darkness she sensed the cruelty of his smile. Satisfied that his point had been made, he put space between them although still holding on to the wilting body that would have crumpled if support had been denied.

'Just a taste of what you must forfeit,' he mocked before stressing the command. 'There must be no repetition of tonight's performance! In future you will remain within the boundaries of the estate and at no time will Doctor Sherlock be allowed admittance. Is that understood?'

Elise would have promised anything to be rid of the autocratic brigand who, whatever else she might profess, could make or break her heart merely by crooking his little finger. Teardrops were glistening on her lashes when she nodded, but he had lost interest in baiting and merely drawled, 'Good! Now I'll take you home and when I return I will inform *le docteur* personally that so far as you are concerned only I hold a licence to love!'

argued it quietly like a good girl—' he said.

CHAPTER TEN

EITHER from motives of mistrust or because of a belated sense of duty, Jacques began spending much more time at the Grand House. Banana and sugar plantations formed an extensive part of the estate and although previously the running of them had been left in the hands of competent managers, Elise was delighted when he began showing signs of interest in affairs of business. She never hesitated to ride with him around the estate when asked—however casually flung the invitation.

She especially loved to watch rum being made by the old pot-still method, and insisted upon having explained every detail as step by step they followed the progress of sugar cane from field to factory. Patiently, Jacques answered her many questions, displaying such a thorough knowledge of his subject that she felt first surprised, then ashamed of having believed him too uninterested to care about the basics of the business founded by an early ancestor.

'The story of rum is the story of sugar,' he told her as lazily they jogged on horseback around the perimeter of the cane fields. 'Its origin goes back to time unrecorded. It is thought that rum was probably first made popular by the invading armies of Genghis Khan—even in Solomon's discourses with the Queen of Sheba there are references to what's thought to be rum.'

Elise, who as a schoolgirl had hated having to learn history, nevertheless loved delving into the past. 'Just imagine!' she breathed, her eyes reflecting dreams, 'Mark Antony might have sipped cool rum sours while his barge floated down the Nile ...'

'And Cleopatra's bathwater might have been half milk, half rum punch!' he jested, his lips twitching more than halfway towards a smile.

'Wasn't it Columbus who was responsible for bringing sugar cane to the West Indies?' she aired her scanty knowledge, wishing she had paid more attention to her lessons.

'It was,' he agreed, controlling a quirk of amusement. 'English sailors of the day called the liquor "Rumbowling" which name gradually became contracted to rum. *"This rum,"* old records state, *"is made of sugar cannes distilled, a hotte hellish and terrible liquor!"*'

'Probably that's why pirates liked it so much—I suppose it complemented their hotte, hellish and terrible passions,' she commented flippantly, then grimaced, wondering if his frown was an indication that her words had been taken as a personal affront to his ancestors.

She sighed relief when his reply pointed to a different train of thought. 'It is providential that as a medium of exchange its power has diminished. In the old days so many slaves were priced at a barrel of rum, so much land for so many puncheons. How many tots would you have fetched when the slave trade was at its height?' he wondered, eyeing her impassively.

She winced, feeling she was being weighed and

found wanting. 'Let's follow the carts to the factory!' she suggested, spurring on her horse in the hope that a change of speed might channel his thoughts away from the unhappy past into an as yet untapped future.

She felt hot and dishevelled by the time they reached the factory and she accepted gratefully the frosted glass of pineapple fizz offered indoors by the manager, Anton Ferrier, who expressed himself much satisfied by their arrival. 'If it was at your instigation that the Comte decided to pay us a visit then I am most grateful,' he beamed upon Elise. 'Of late he has been most neglectful, but now that I have met you, Madame la Comtesse, I can well understand, and forgive his very natural desire to spend every available moment with his beautiful bride!'

Elise was conscious of Jacques' start of surprise. Recently, many compliments had come her way and she would not have been feminine had she not enjoyed the unaccustomed praise. Of course, compared with Camilla she was a non-starter, but even so, Jacques had no right to be staring at her in such an unflattering way!

His attitude drove her into replying more warmly than the compliment merited. Setting down her empty glass, she walked across to the startled manager and slipped a hand into the crook of his elbow. 'I have been looking forward enormously to having you show me round the factory, Anton. You don't mind if I call you Anton ...?'

'I am honoured, Madame la Comtesse!'

'Elise, please ...' she begged with an enslaving

smile. 'Then can we begin our tour now? I'm sure my husband will find plenty to occupy him until our return.'

'Indeed, yes—to both questions,' Anton Ferrier assured her, still reeling from the impact of her smile. 'Our chief accountant has much he wishes to discuss with Monsieur le Comte, so if he will excuse us?' he enquired of Jacques as Elise began edging him towards the door.

The bemused man was not aware, as he steered her around the factory, that her smiles owed as much to satisfaction as to interest. She listened carefully as he outlined how the cane was put through crushers and rollers to extract the juice which was then pumped into large tanks to be heated, clarified, then allowed to settle; seemed utterly absorbed in the process of decanting the juice into evaporators and vacuum pans, and made all the right remarks when viewing the enormous vats in which gallons of the resulting molasses had been left to ferment. But Jacques' expression of tight-lipped displeasure remained with her all during the tour; it was a new experience for him to be relegated to the background and an unexpected rebuff to the condescension he had shown when issuing the invitation in the first place.

The manager was gratified by her insistence upon being shown everything, even though by the time he had finished all the workers had gone home and the only car remaining outside of the offices was his own.

'Time sprouts wings when the hours are pleasant, Madame Elise,' he sighed, anxiously scanning his watch. 'I hope Monsieur will forgive me for mono-polizing your company.'

'Don't worry, the fault is mine and I will tell him so. Ah, here he comes now! Goodbye, and thank you, Anton, for a most interesting afternoon.' Quickly Elise mounted the mare that had docilely trotted up to her while Jacques, who was already in the saddle, waited in obvious black humour.

'Please return soon!' Anton called out as the horses broke into a canter.

'Thank you, I will!' she called back, feeling slightly apprehensive of the unbending rigidity of her husband's spine.

They had ridden in silence past the patchwork of cane fields, through rolling parklands and had begun climbing the forest trail leading upwards to the house when Elise decided that now was as good a time as any to broach the subject that would give her mind no rest.

She was riding slightly ahead of Jacques, so she reined in her horse and slid to the ground, block-ing his progress along the narrow tree-lined path. He dismounted, sharply questioning, 'What's wrong, is it your mount?'

'Nothing's wrong,' she returned with a level stare, 'but there is something we must discuss.'

'There is?' The sudden arch of his eyebrows was intimidating, but she refused to be cowed. A fallen tree lay embedded in a clearing of ferns and she moved towards it, her expression unconsciously pleading as she suggested: 'Let's sit down, it may take me a while to explain.'

With a shrug that indicated his opinion of the

vagaries of women, he decided to humour her. The silence was unnerving as he waited, flicking his whip against a booted leg, watching with interest the beautiful violet and orange tail-spread of a nearby humming bird. As a preliminary, she cleared her suddenly parched throat, then stammering slightly with nervousness she began, 'Our marriage was an act of great irresponsibility on both our parts ...'

His head swivelled. 'I believe that fact has already been established.'

'Yes, but there's no reason why we should suffer for the rest of our lives because of it!' she hurried on, desperate to state her case before his clinical observations could begin slicing into her arguments. 'You insist you're in love with Camilla and she with you. Well, if that's so, she won't mind waiting for as long as it might take to have our marriage annulled.'

The plaintive, lonely whistle of a solitaire thrush filled the clearing, an astonished sound, the breathless trill of a shocked, unwilling eavesdropper.

Jacques did not wait to deliberate, his answer came bullet-swift, shot with steel. 'Spare me the deception of pretending that my welfare is your only consideration! Annulment would suit you very well, I've no doubt. Even in these enlightened days, doctors still have to be extremely careful not to allow any suspicion of scandal to mar their professional standing.'

'I don't know what you mean ...' she wavered.

'Come now,' he derided, 'you usually have a superb grasp of the obvious!' With one slash of his riding crop he decapitated a spray of yellow blossom popularly named 'shamer' because of its ability to fold up and hide at the slightest touch. At that moment Elise would have given anything to have been able to do the same.

'As I've already said, Jeremy is nothing more than a friend,' she insisted with dignity. 'If there was, or indeed were ever likely to be, anything more serious between us I would tell you now. But although I feel happy in his company—wildly so, at times,' she admitted incautiously, 'he's too much in love with Camilla to spare me a thought.' A quick intake of air hissed through flared nostrils was Jacques' reaction to the remark voiced with wistful innocence. Reading jealousy in the action, she jerked out, 'Don't worry, he knows it's hopeless, he's perfectly well aware how you and Camilla feel about each other,' she assured him, her large eyes liquid with concern.

She could not fathom the derision behind his tight smile, nor the depth of anger darkening his blue eyes. 'It is a mistake to underestimate one's opponents,' he muttered through teeth bared as in the smile of a tiger. 'The good *docteur* will need to be watched even more closely than I first thought.'

He needed only the slightest encouragement to become preoccupied with thoughts of Camilla, Elise fumed, feeling the conversation was getting them nowhere. Impatient of being sidetracked, she demanded, 'Well, will you have our marriage annulled or not?'

'No!' he supplied briefly without hesitation,

his look chilling the colour from her cheeks.

She stared with wide distressed eyes. Behind him ferns sprouted high, stretching to outreach neighbouring trees that towered above their frail competitors; she felt her strength was just as pitifully inadequate against his implacable decision. 'But why . . . ?' she finally appealed, aching to know why he wished to retain the only obstacle barring his way to freedom.

Jacques stood up and stretched—like a lazy, satisfied panther, she thought, replete, yet too acquisitive to relinquish unwanted prey! As if sensing the applied simile, he growled a deep-throated laugh and mocked her timidity, *Pauvre petite souris!* If you wish to indulge in a surfeit of cheese you must accept the confines of the trap!'

Later, within the cool splendour of her bedroom, Elise had to agree that she was indeed a mouse caught in a gilded, luxurious trap. Many would have envied her her view of velvet lawns encircling fountains spraying cool water into marble basins, and the sea of forest and green pastures flowing unceasingly as far as the eye could see from the balcony of a house perched halfway up the side of a mountain. Such a house deserved a chatelaine with the aplomb of a duchess, Elise meditated, stroking heavy velvet drapes with restless hands. Camilla would fit perfectly into the majestic setting designed by artists to accommodate the *aristocratie*. She sighed, knowing she could never emulate the graceful ease with which Camilla sauntered through life—controlled in pleasure, controlled in anger, controlled even in *love*. She winced. She herself tackled pleasure with vital enthusiasm, in anger she could be downright wicked, and in love . . .! She blushed, honestly acknowledging the fact that given the chance to love she would be vitally enthusiastic, downright wicked and probably sinfully abandoned!

There was to be a dinner party that evening—her first public ordeal as mistress of the Grand House. Jacques had invited Camilla, Janine and their father to dinner and when he had casually dropped the bombshell a few days earlier her panic-stricken expression had seemed to afford him much amusement.

'You will cope perfectly,' he had assured her with typical masculine blindness. 'Mattie is the best cook on the island.' This was perfectly true, but presentation was almost as important as content and in this department there was no one to whom she could turn for either advice or encouragement. Although seemingly unconcerned, she knew he was depending upon her to ensure that the dinner party was a success—sensitive to the fact that previous efforts to entertain at the Grand House had resulted in dismal culinary failures.

She dressed unhurriedly, determined not to become flustered or to be tempted into checking yet again arrangements planned to the last detail days previously. In the kitchen Mattie reigned supreme; she had no worries whatever about the outcome of the menu they had both agreed should satisfy even the most epicurean of tastes. Silver and crystal had been polished until the ensuing shine was hurtful to the eyes when the sun caught its surface, and a dinner service of delicate china, stamped with the family crest, had been complemented with carefully selected place mats and napery of finest lawn.

She chose a white dress, a sleeveless sheath, puritanical in contrast with her previous startling outfits, its high neckline cut across with the uncompromising straightness of a child's pinafore. Beneath hair brushed silken smooth, her face reflected the solemnity of the occasion; worried eyes, furrowed brow, and lips a protesting red from the onslaught of gnawing teeth. She was ready a full hour before their guests were due to arrive, so resisting once more the temptation to meddle, she went downstairs, gravitating instinctively towards her den, the one place in the house where she could completely relax.

She had been inside only a few minutes when Jacques sought her out. Looking debonair and vitally attractive in a white dinner jacket, slim black slacks and a shirt of finely tucked linen, he sauntered in, a black tie dangling from impatient fingers.

'I can't get this damned thing to stay put!' he proffered the offending tie. 'Will you try?'

Elise had to stand on tiptoe to reach around his neck and when she staggered he clutched her waist to steady her. Obediently, he heeded her instruction to hold still while she tied the knot, fumbling beneath his branding hold.

'There!' She gasped with relief when the tie settled satisfactorily, but when she made to withdraw he held her captive.

'Little Quaker!' His smile held devastating charm. 'You once declared that a man becomes a creature of his uniform—can I surmise from the demureness of your dress that tonight you do not intend being as flirtatious as usual?'

'I have never flirted,' she muttered, suffocated by his nearness, 'but in any case, tonight's guests would render my choice limited.'

'*Tiens*, my memory!' He smote his brow. 'I'm sorry, I ought to have mentioned earlier that there will be one more guest for dinner. Camilla prevailed upon my good nature and coaxed me to invite Jeremy Sherlock. Seemingly five is an awkward number at the dinner table,' he continued, watching her keenly. 'According to Camilla, as hostess, you will welcome Jeremy's presence with relief?'

She tried to escape, hoping to move nonchalantly out of his clutches to a safe distance, but he was equally determined to keep her prisoner until she supplied the answer to his question.

'As usual, you seem determined to read more into my friendship with Jeremy than has ever existed,' she accused, working up anger in an attempt to combat a weakness at the knees and a terrible yearning to press her lips against his firm mouth. 'But even that doesn't excuse your treating me like a prisoner,' she charged. 'For weeks now I haven't been allowed to set foot outside of the estate without being shadowed! Why? Don't you trust me? I've given my promise to behave, isn't that enough?'

'No, it is not enough!' he retorted. 'Before, whenever you were left alone I was on tenterhooks wondering what you were up to and where and when you would appear. Every time I looked around, it seemed, you appeared at my elbow dressed either as a shabby urchin or wearing gear so outrageous that the capital was shaken to its foundations!'

'I *never* followed you ...!' she flashed.

'I might have felt easier if you had, at least then I would have known where and when to expect you. No,' he decided, 'you will remain under my eye until I can be certain of your actions—if ever,' he breathed, sighting a gleam of rebellion. Then to appease her into a less fiery state of mind before their guests arrived, he attempted to pacify, 'In any case, what's so wrong about a husband monopolizing his wife? Who knows,' he glittered, 'togetherness might become a habit we'll be loath to break.'

Remembering his angry denouncement of her trickery, his cruel revenge, and his very obvious desire for Camilla, Elise blurted out, 'That would be intolerable!'

'Why do you say that?' he snapped back.

Tears spurted, a weakness brought about by the tension of the past few hours, her unsureness of being able to handle her responsibilities as hostess and most of all the strain of having to endure so much torment wrung from her soul. She heard Jacques' muttered curse when tears she could not check began trickling down her cheeks, and sensed that far from encouraging pity, the sight of them had moved him to unaccountable rage. There was heartbreak in her voice when she supplied the answer he was demanding.

'Because ... because you hardly ever smile ...'

'I can't afford to yet,' he clenched.

'Will you ever?' she sobbed.

Their glances clung and she was the first to look away. 'Perhaps when we say goodbye,' he punished her deliberately, 'finally say goodbye. But that may not be for some time yet. If I cannot have the woman I want, I must make do with the woman I have!'

'Will you ever?' she sobbed.
Their glances clung and she was the first to look
away. 'Perhaps when we say goodbye,' he punished

CHAPTER ELEVEN

PEPPERPOT soup, served creamy and very hot, delighted the palate of Camilla's father and put him in a thoroughly good humour to enjoy scalloped mountain crayfish followed by roast duckling with a piquant stuffing, then a dessert specially concocted by Mattie in honour of the occasion.

'How can I be expected to control puppy fat when I'm deliberately enticed from my diet?' Janine wailed, scooping up the last delicious spoonful of rum cream iced around a selection of chopped island fruits.

Delicately, Camilla laid down her spoon, leaving half of her sweet course untouched. 'You really are the most awful glutton.' She directed her sister a look of distaste. 'Tomorrow you'll probably be rolling in agony complaining of stomach ache and making life unbearable for everyone!'

Janine resisted the urge to reply equally unkindly. Camilla had been looking forward enormously to this dinner party, but for some reason her enjoyment had become blighted immediately she had entered the dining salon and scanned the glittering, beautifully appointed table. Her displeasure was puzzling. No one could possibly find fault with the arrangement of antique silver cutlery reflecting the soft glow of lighted candles that rose like slender towers from mauve, blue and purple flowers clustered around their base. Crystal goblets with silver mounts, that tinkled finely at the touch of a fingernail, made potent excitement out of each sip of wine, and each course, served on plate designed to delight fastidious nobility, was a masterpiece of the culinary art.

One small frown of disapproval towards his elder daughter was all Camilla's father allowed himself before relaxing, replete, to congratulate his hostess. 'I've travelled thousands of miles in my lifetime, Comtesse, but never before have I enjoyed such a wonderful meal—nor one so tastefully served. Congratulations, my dear—and you, too, Jacques, for having the sense to choose a wife who is as accomplished as she is beautiful.'

Elise acknowledged the compliment, avoiding after one quick glance the startling pleasure of her husband's smile. Colour flooded her cheeks at the thought of having pleased him and lashes swept down to screen a sparkle of joy.

'I must confess Elise is full of surprises,' idly tolerant, he made the admission. 'I am constantly being either scandalized or amazed by my wife's actions.'

'Then you are doubly blessed, *monsieur*,' Jeremy observed dryly. 'To have a lifetime of stimulating partnership ahead of you is to be greatly envied.'

'Envied by whom?' Jacques countered, swift as a drawn sword. 'To envy is to covet! Are you admitting that you covet my wife, *monsieur*?'

Ignoring the steel, Jeremy grasped the velvet glove. 'Indeed I do, *monsieur*, any lone bachelor such as myself could not do otherwise!'

There was an intense awareness of conflict when

Jacques rose to suggest with bare politeness that the men should retire into the library for brandy while coffee was served to the ladies in the small salon. No one objected, but uneasy glances were exchanged as silently they withdrew from the table to proceed to their allotted stations. Elise tried to intervene, whispering to Jacques as he escorted her across the hall, 'I worked hard to ensure the success of this dinner party—I will not have you spoiling it by being discourteous to a guest!'

Too late, the disdainful flare of his nostrils warned that she had transgressed. *How dared she tell the Comte de Montague to mind his manners!*

'You are beginning to sound uncomfortably like a nagging wife!' was his terse reply, projected through lips drawn into the shape of a smile which fooled nobody, least of all Elise, who was too near to escape the cool deadliness of his aim. She shrugged, wearied by his unreasonable resentment of Jeremy. He did not want her himself, but neither should any other man. However often she insisted there was nothing between them the more convinced he became that there was. A hundred years ago a duel would have been the answer—a sword-fight to the death to prove one man's right to retain sole possession of his woman. At this very moment Jacques would revel in such release, but not Jeremy —his cultured outlook, his modern views on the liberation of women, his scorn of violence and his reliance upon the spoken word were flints to Jacques' tinder!

Mattie served the coffee herself, anxious to know how her efforts had been received, and left the salon delighted by unstinted praise. But Janine was restless, her eyes moving from one object to another in a feast of admiration. 'Do you mind if I skip coffee and just wander around for a while?' she begged, wanting to unearth further treasures.

Elise was nonplussed; there was a gleam in Camilla's eyes she did not trust and Janine's absence could be the opportunity she was waiting for to begin an inquisition. 'Wouldn't you rather wait until Jacques is ready to show you round—he's so knowledgeable about the contents of the house you're sure to find the tour more interesting in his company?'

'Oh, let her go!' Camilla exerted gentle pressure, 'Janine is the most unrelaxed person I know, and after that excellent dinner I feel in need of an interlude of peace before the men rejoin us. Run along, darling,' she insisted lazily, draping her graceful body across an elegant settee.

Nervously, Elise manipulated the coffee pot, sensing eyes following her every movement. It was a relief when the small exercise was accomplished without mishap and she was able to relax in her chair feeling a small sense of triumph. Her victory was short-lived, however. Camilla was not one to procrastinate, but even so the bluntness of her approach rendered Elise breathless.

'You must be feeling very pleased with yourself —compliments from the male members of our party have rained down thick and fast upon your demure little head! How do you do it, I wonder?' As Elise squirmed under her unflattering look, Camilla leant forward to emphasize, 'I know you tricked

Jacques into marrying you, just as I also know that although you may think yourself safe the marriage is doomed to failure! Jacques loves me, I can't tell you how many times he has held me in his arms, pouring out words of desire, yearning and *need* ...!'

Elise jumped to her feet, agitated beyond belief by the betrayal. 'But he never proposed!' she jerked without thought, angry with Jacques for placing her in such a humiliating position.

Camilla's patrician features overran with colour; the reminder an ever-pricking thorn. 'He would have,' she defended, 'had you not played upon his chivalry and forced him into accepting responsibility for your future! Marriage is rather a high price to have to pay for a little hospitality and the company of a scheming old woman and a clinging child!'

Elise rounded on her, furiously angered by the slur on her grandmother. 'How dare you refer in such a contemptuous way to my grandmother—she was as incapable of scheming as I am of clinging! If Jacques has told you so much, then let him also tell you why he has refused my request to have our marriage annulled. Far from being eager to escape, he's hugging his bonds, following me about so closely I'm prevented from even speaking to any other man. You need only recall his reaction to Jeremy's harmless compliment over dinner to prove that what I say is true. Like his acquisitive ancestors, Jacques is loath to relinquish any article branded with his name!'

Camilla stood her ground. 'His reasons are obvious,' she stated calmly. 'He has always been greatly concerned with family honour and is probably ensuring that you're given no chance to supply more ammunition to the island's army of gossips. I'm prepared to accept that for the moment the marriage must stand—and I *can* accept it,' she smiled thinly, 'knowing it's a marriage in name only, knowing also that I possess his heart, his loyalty, his every thought, whereas you have to be content with an empty bed.' Her composure lost some of its brittleness when, with a rustle of silk, she leant forward to sneer, 'Make the most of the little you have, my dear, because very shortly you're going to have to make way for me!'

Elise turned away from taunting eyes that would have relished the sight of her agony. For seconds she remained with her eyes closed, then when the battle for control had been won tear-heavy lashes lifted just in time to see Mattie backing out of the open doorway, her usually smile-drenched face so crumpled Elise knew that every word of Camilla's last damaging statement had been overheard. Dismayed by the old servant's distress, she sped across the hall in her wake, but before she could catch her up the library door opened and the men appeared.

Jacques strode forward, questioning her solitary presence amid the gloom of the great hall where battle pennants hung like tattered ribbons against rough grey walls and tongues of orange and red flame cast from the open fireplace reflected eerily upon suits of armour ranged stiffly around the room darkened by an imminent storm. Elise looked as lost and out of place as a damsel on a battlefield, a solitary, white-clad wraith seeking to separate friend from foe. Jeremy seemed a natural choice and it was to him she turned for protection against Jacques' hurtful coolness.

'Janine is exploring the house, would you like to do the same?' she jerked, not realizing how urgency had turned the question into an appeal.

'I intend showing our guests around together,' Jacques quelled with a glance.

'I know, but as Camilla is not quite ready, I thought Jeremy and I could keep Janine company until the rest of you join us later.'

'Good idea!' Jeremy sauntered forward, imperturbable as ever, determined to answer the signals of distress flying high in her cheeks. Immensely comforted by his sympathetic awareness of her need, Elise slipped her hand into the bend of his elbow and began guiding him towards the stairs, suppressing shivers of tension brought about by the suspicion that vexed eyes were boring into her back. Not until they had reached the picture gallery did she relax, and then only far enough to expel breath tightly withheld while in Jacques' proximity.

'Your nerves are set on a knife edge.' Jeremy spun her round to face him, tracing the outline of her chin with a caressing thumb. 'Why don't you leave here, Elise?' he urged. 'Sooner or later you're going to have to admit yourself beaten, so why prolong the agony of playing substitute bride when there are others who, given a little encouragement, would willingly take the place of your erring . husband?'

She croaked a laugh, feeling for some reason uneasy. 'I haven't noticed any queue forming!' she quipped, mistrusting the very personal aura building up around them.

Jeremy regarded her steadily. Portraits of earlier Montagues surrounded them, their painted eyes peering, sentry sharp, as if to guard family property against thieving marauders. Her mouth quivered as nervously she glanced around, keenly susceptible to the disapproval emanated by images of haughty, arrogant men who in their lifetime would have thought nothing of running through with a lusty sword any man daring to look at their women in the way Jeremy was looking at her, and proud wives who had known better than to aggravate the tempers of their mettlesome men.

'Hoist by my own petard!' he murmured, pulling her resisting body into his arms.

'Jeremy ... I don't understand!' her voice rose high with surprise.

'The object of the exercise was to make Camilla jealous,' he bent closer, 'but now I find myself thinking only of you, grabbing any excuse to be near you—as I did this evening because I was starved of the sight of your unhappy little face and solemn eyes. I love you!' he murmured thickly, his mouth descending to burn against her throat, '... enchanting ... fey ... desirable little witch!'

For one startled, horrified second Elise was too numbed to move, but as his kisses grew wilder revulsion seared her soul. 'No! Stop! Please, you mustn't ...!' she gasped, straining out of his clutch. But the stranger she had welcomed as a friend was beyond reason, beyond even hearing the tread of footsteps rapidly approaching them up the stairs.

Flushed and wildly dishevelled, she tore out of his arms which once had beckoned as a haven of calm and ran—straight into the arms of her husband, who rounded the corner of the gallery seconds too late to appreciate that she was running to escape and not merely to evade discovery. With one sweeping look he took in the tableau, reading his own meaning into Elise's scarlet cheeks, crumpled dress and disarranged hair.

His appearance had a sobering effect upon Jeremy who, ignoring the explosive atmosphere, reverted to his usual nonchalance. With an ease Elise found amazing, he greeted Jacques with a smile. 'Were you wondering what kept us?' Casually he straightened his tie, 'My fault, I'm afraid, your possessions are so fascinating I could barely tear myself away.'

She gasped at his effrontery, wondering how she could have swum so blithely in such dangerous depths. Never had she suspected him of feeling anything other than sympathy and a mild regard, which was why she had been able to laugh off Jacques' repeated suspicions! Felling in sudden need of protection, she drew closer to Jacques' side, but when his freezing glance swept downward, questioning her daring, she stepped back, suppressing an hysterical desire to giggle as she contemplated the folly of running to the tiger for protection from the lion.

Jacques rocked on his heels, muscles tensed as if prepared to spring, his eyes flashing a murderous desire to revenge the insult to which, as yet, he had given no name. Infidelity! Adultery! Unfaithfulness! Which one would he choose, she wondered wearily, feeling too defeated to care.

But when finally he addressed Jeremy his voice was modulated, the fury churning within his lean frame carefully contained. 'Camilla has a headache, she wishes to return to her hotel. As you brought them here in your car, perhaps you would be good enough to drive them back?'

Jeremy's wary stance relaxed. 'Of course, we'll leave immediately,' he breezed. Not entirely without conscience, however, he hesitated before passing Elise and would probably have lingered long enough to offer an apology had not Jacques sped him on his way with a terse farewell.

'*Bonne nuit, monsieur!*'

'*Au revoir*,' Jeremy contradicted, his eyes upon Elise's bent head, '... until we meet again.'

She remained motionless, expecting a scornful diatribe to begin immediately Jeremy was out of earshot, but silence followed his retreating footsteps and when she finally nerved herself to look she found to her amazement that she was completely alone. Relief pounded through her veins as timidly she peered into gloomy corners and found them empty of Jacques' terrifying presence. Stumbling at first, then with gathering speed, she began to run and did not stop until she gained her bedroom and had banged shut the door against the menace she felt was creeping, pressing, *threatening* all around her.

An hour later a tap upon her door set dormant nerves quivering, but it was Mattie's voice that begged admittance in reply to her ragged: 'Who's there?'

'Just a second!' she commanded in lacklustre tone as she dragged herself from the bed on which for the past hour she had lain in a state of numbed stupor, assessing the various forms her inevitable punishment might take. She could withstand anything, she had decided, except the torture in which Jacques excelled—physical hatemaking—that soul-destroying storm of kissing, caressing and mocking murmurings, glaring with deceit, yet powerfully destructive of feminine defences. She dared not let her mind linger too long upon her last sight of Jacques, his imperious features stamped with dark passionate anger and some other emotion to which she could put no name. Hurt, disillusionment, jealousy—all of these she rejected as emotions alien to the imperturbable Comte—and yet ... A sob tore from her throat as fiercely she dismissed such possibilities. What he had seen, or rather, what he thought he had seen, had dealt a severe blow to his pride—no more. Yet to a man of such arrogance the act was enough to merit the severest of revenge. Thank heaven, she breathed, centuries had passed since men had gained satisfaction by running their enemies through with blades of cold steel. And chastised wives had been condemned to suffer the discomfort of imprisonment in some cold, isolated tower ...

By the time she was admitted, Mattie was consumed with anxiety. 'Why you dun locked your door, Missie Elise?' she questioned as she entered, her worried eyes darkening as they scoured a pale, ravaged face and woeful but disturbed eyes.

'No reason . . .' Elise faltered, unable to summon the energy to frame a plausible excuse.

Mattie's scowl was frightening. 'Dat Camilla ain't no good, she's gonna try to be mistress of this house! Massa Jacques is one big fool, I think!'

Elise turned away to hide the pain flickering across her features. 'I'm the fool, Mattie. Jacques has loved Camilla for a very long time and would have made her his wife but for my intervention. Love cannot be dismissed to order, as I very well know. If it's real it's lasting.' The utter dejection on Mattie's face caused her a pang and quickly she tried to comfort. 'But you're not to worry your head about my problems—if ever I have to leave I'll take you with me, Mattie, I promise.'

Mattie's expression lightened fractionally, then encouraged by the more cheerful note she sidled up to Elise and produced a twist of blue paper from out of her apron pocket. 'No need to leave, missie, if you make use of this Massa Jacques'll be the lovinest husband on the whole island!'

Elise stared at the screw of paper. 'What is it?' she whispered, needing her suspicions confirmed.

'A love potion!' Mattie's gleeful chuckle filled the room. 'I dun paid the obeah man two chickens an' a cask of rum fer it, an' he swears I'll get em all back if the potion don' work!'

Firmly, Elise brought her down to earth. By rights, she ought to have scolded Mattie severely for becoming involved in a practice outlawed many years before, but the gesture had been motivated by love, a commodity in very short supply. 'Burn it at

144

once, Mattie! The powder contained in that piece of paper is a dangerous drug and if you're caught with it in your possession you could be in very serious trouble! Oh, I know,' she waved away Mattie's protest, 'you islanders have used such potions for hundreds of years, but still you have no way of knowing what harm might have been done. You're like children unaware of the danger of playing with an unexploded bomb. How many times have you seen men and women dancing themselves into a frenzy after indulging in the obeah man's potions? How many have fallen exhausted to the ground, sat half-demented in the branches of trees, or ran about with arms outstretched convinced that they were about to fly?'

'Jus' in fun ...' Mattie muttered sulkily.

'Dope!' Elise insisted firmly, 'banned, illegal dope which must never again be brought inside this house, do you understand?'

With a feeling of unease, Elise noted Mattie's protruding bottom lip and rebellious expression. Having roots buried deep in folklore, Mattie would take a lot of convincing that the homespun remedies extracted from local plants could be as harmful as she had just claimed. When weariness descended like a cloud, Elise decided to abandon the subject until such time she might feel capable of explaining more fully the dangers of narcotics to the old servant who possessed a stubbornness typical of her race.

'I must sleep now, Mattie, I'm very tired. We'll talk again in the morning, but meanwhile get rid of that powder—if Jacques discovers it he'll be after your hide!'

round to search the shadows for its cause. It had
sounded like a squeaking door handle being slowly
turned. But who would want to enter her room at

CHAPTER TWELVE

WELL after midnight Elise abandoned all hope of
sleep. Aching with tiredness, she slid her feet into
slippers of soft kid and belted a filmy blue negligée
around her slender waist. Hours of tossing and
turning had resulted in hair tousled as a child's,
clinging in damp tendrils against a pale brow and
into the tender nape of her neck before tumbling
in a cascade almost to her waist. She walked across
to the window, but found no comfort in the sight
of heavy rainclouds scudding across a sky of copper
plate. The storm that had threatened all day was
now imminent, all living creatures were quiet and
still, cowering in fear from sharp tongues of lightning striking the copper sky, flame against metal. It
was as if the whole universe was waiting for a battle
to begin, she thought uneasily, shivering even
though a clammy blast of heat was pressing its way
through open windows.

Hugging herself for comfort, she leant against
the massive window-frame, wincing at each lightning flash, trembling through each thunderous
rumble, hardly daring to breathe as each second
advanced the moment of eruption of savage elements that would have to be endured before peace
could once more reign.

When a sound impinged the quietness of the
room she barely paid it any attention, but when it
came again, louder and more decisive, she swung

round to search the shadows for its cause. It had sounded like a squeaking door handle being slowly turned. But who would want to enter her room at this hour? All the servants would be sleeping and not even Mattie would venture inside unless called.

A gasp of fear wedged in her throat when a patch of shadow moved. 'Who's there?' she called out sharply, feeling sweat beading her brow.

Her answer was a low, throaty laugh. 'A strange question from a new bride!' was the mocking reply. 'Who else but your husband could expect to find a welcome in your bedroom at this hour?'

'*Jacques!*' His name tore raggedly from her tongue.

As he sauntered forward lightning flashed and for a split second his domineering figure was glaringly outlined, the deep tones of his silken robe, rich red, indigo blue, leaping suddenly to life. He was at one with the leashed elements, his turbulence smothered by an unnatural calm, with all around him a menacing aura of havoc yet to come.

When he reached her Elise saw that his eyes were as slumbrous as the becalmed ocean—and as dangerously deceptive. Panic-stricken, she stepped back, only to find her retreat blocked by a solid wall, her only other escape route leading to the confined space of an outside balcony. 'What do you want?' she questioned bravely, but with shaking knees.

He answered by reaching out to grasp her shoulder and slowly, carelessly, smoothing his fingers along the length of her arm with a sensuous possessiveness that set her nerves screaming. 'What you seem prepared to offer any man who finds you attractive,' he informed her hatefully, his eyes cold.

'Please,' she sounded as stifled as she felt, 'don't play games with me ... !'

Her chin was guided by rough fingers until she was forced to meet his languorous eyes. 'No such frivolous intention has crossed my mind, *chérie*. My presence here can be classed as being purely business.'

'Business ... ?' she choked, as repetitive as a parrot.

'The business of teaching a wife to love, honour and obey her husband,' he stressed silkily, his fingers cruelly jerking her head when she tried to turn away.

'You're hurting me!' she pleaded when the pressure of his fingers threated to snap her jaw. In desperation, she tried to explain. 'I know what you must have thought when you saw Jeremy and me together, but I swear I had no idea how he felt—'

'Be quiet!' The command snapped through lips wire-taut. 'Don't dare lie to me! Do you imagine I am blind, deaf and insensitive as well as a fool!' Startled by his venom, Elise stared, her quivering lips falling open like slowly parting petals. Fear paralysed her limbs. His eyes had a brooding, almost insane quality, his reckless manner reminiscent of someone under the influence of drink—*or drugs!*

Dear God!' she moaned, suddenly reminded of Mattie's shocking suggestion. Jacques always had a nightcap in his study before going to bed. The servants had been instructed to ensure that the drinks tray was amply stocked and Mattie had formed the habit of checking that everything was in order each evening before she retired. *Could she have ...?* Had she *dared* succumb to the temptation of drugging his drink even after the dire threats that had been poured upon her head?

Agitated beyond reason, she decided to attempt to explain and when the pressure of his arms pulled her forward she protested but did not physically resist. 'Jacques, you're not yourself, why don't you——' The rest of her words were smothered by a kiss that blotted out all thought, a kiss so devastating she could do no more than clutch convulsively at the lapels of his robe while the ground disappeared from beneath her feet and she was left spinning in mid-air, helpless in the core of an emotional whirlwind. 'Jacques ...!' she tore her lips free, 'listen to me ...!'

'Why? So that you can tell me that you love me, *have* always and *will* always love me?' he jeered. 'Don't waste your breath on such meaningless lies, *chérie*, I know that any honest, lasting relationship between the sexes is impossible, therefore the satisfying of physical hunger must take its place. Meanwhile, little faker, you must drop this pretence of modesty, because never again will you find me idiot enough to wait for signs of maturity in a seeming child who behind my back has been amusing herself by practising a harlot's skill upon other men! Begin practising on your husband, *mon ange*,' he derided, burying cruel lips against the velvet softness of her throat, enjoying her gasp of pain, feeling gratified by heartbroken tears that were helping to wash the sting of mortification from his scarred pride.

His brutal chastisement was worse than any she had previously endured. No hint of tenderness was betrayed in lips that explored every vulnerable curve and hollow of her neck and shoulders; no desire was contained in false endearments mocked against her thrashed mouth and against the sensitive lobes of her ears; no gentleness in hands that caressed with masterly skill until eventually the barriers of her restraint were stormed, leaving her vulnerable to a surge of demanding passion.

The stirring of the elements outdoors was a fitting accompaniment to the physical and mental combat taking place inside the room which over the centuries had secreted many such escapades between virile master and reluctant maid. The Montague men of past eras had been brigands, renowned for their daring, admired for their courage and proud of their reputation of being able to entice fiery response from the iciest of *novices*.

'Ma coquette angélique!' His throaty laugh was muffled as his lips enclosed a nerve frantically pulsating in the hollow of her throat. The humorous jibe penetrated her euphoria, stabbing straight to the heart of her passion, awakening her with a jolt to the realization that her shy abandonment was affording him much amusement. Heat of humiliation supplied strength not previously forthcoming which, together with the element of surprise, was responsible for the success of the violent push that freed her from his arms.

Panting with fear, she flung herself across the room until the breadth of the enormous bed was between them, then, wild-eyed and dishevelled, she glared towards his advancing figure and choked out the threat, 'If you come any nearer I'll scream the house down!'

All was silent as, rocking slightly on his heels, Jacques considered her ultimatum. With the keenness of a tiger stalking prey, he narrowly judged the distance separating them, then, assessing the chances of a rush attack too slim, he reverted to the subtlety of reproach. The injury he projected in his soft accusation plucked a response from her quivering heartstrings.

'Must I remind you of our bargain—security for you, and for myself the stability of a wife and family? Am I to understand that having fulfilled my part of the agreement you intend welching on yours?'

Elise stared into his sardonic face, hating the ease with which he had so neatly put her in the wrong and the air of regret which, although certainly false, had the effect of making her feel decidedly guilty. If only he would listen to reason, she thought wildly, but the potion she was now sure Mattie had administered was numbing to the brain as well as exhilarating to the senses, which rendered the employment of logic useless.

He was becoming impatient, every muscle tensed as if to spring, so to delay his attack she nervously began to plead, 'Please, Jacques, go back to your room! I can never take Camilla's place in your heart and I no longer want to try. Besides,' her voice broke, 'by morning you'll wonder what madness caused you to think me desirable enough to want to consummate a marriage which represents the only barrier between yourself and freedom ...'

To her great relief he seemed to accept her argument. Gradually, he relaxed his watchful stance and slumped slowly down on to the bed, cradling his bowed head in his hands, creating a picture of dejection that was immediately disarming.

'Have you any idea what loneliness means—not just the conventional word, but the naked terror?' she could barely hear the muffled question. 'Am I a monster, doomed to a solitary existence on condition of having every possession one could wish to own?'

Grief-stricken, she ran to him, stumbling in her haste to reach the man whose slumped body epitomized bleak despair. She dropped to her knees, coiling an arm around his shoulders in a demonstration of compassion, and sobbed out the promise, 'You'll always have me! I'll stay with you for ever even if,' she gulped, 'I have to share you with Camilla! You'll never be alone again ...'

His head remained averted from the earnest face with gamin features coloured honey brown by the sun, topaz eyes swimming with love, and a soft mouth still quivering from an onslaught of brutal kisses yet anxious to frame words of forgiveness and love. When he did not move she placed cool young lips against the hand screening his face and whispered, 'I know how sensitive you are about the lies that have been told about you, but please try to forget them,' she urged, full of compassion for the man whose arrogant self-assurance was no more than a blind drawn across his over-susceptible feelings. 'I believe in you—not even Grand'mère could shake my faith in you when she warned me about some scandal involving a girl in Paris. I know you're incapable of being deliberately unkind,' she finished, her simplicity utterly convincing.

'So you know about the girl in Paris ...?'

Her arms tightened around him in a spasm of comfort. 'Forget her! Remember only that I married you not for reasons of money, security or position, but because I adore you, life would be a desert without you!' Tenderly she stroked his hand and waited for his reaction to the outpourings of her secret soul, feeling soaring elation at having at last penetrated the depths of the complex man matured out of the stresses and strains imposed upon an uncomplicated boy. The future seemed to beckon, promising a lifetime of laughter and love such as they had shared so many years ago.

When Jacques dropped his hands and lifted his head she stared, transfixed, the smile fading slowly from lips growing suddenly chilled as she became aware of the devilry in his white-toothed smile. She had no need of the swift grasp of fingers around her wrist to warn her that she had been tricked. Instinct told her just a split second before his triumphant: '*Naïve enfant!*' spelled out the treachery of his deed.

Pinned to his side by the edge of the bed, she scorned to struggle and matched his look of satisfaction with one of pride. Not that she had much pride to spare. The memory of her childish outpourings were as galling as the deception he had employed to send her grovelling at his feet with the eagerness of an adoring slave.

'Did you really think to escape punishment so easily?' he murmured, content to bide his time now his trap was sprung.

'I should have known better than to expect compassion from a corsair!' she replied, bitterly condemning of the looting of her innermost feelings.

Black hair took on the blue sheen of a raven when he threw back his head and laughed. 'Fickle woman! A moment ago you assured me I was incapable of being unkind!'

'*Deliberately* unkind,' she corrected, hesitant to incur his wrath upon Mattie's head by spelling out the suspicion in her mind.

'Am I being forced against my will, then ...?' he jeered, exerting pressure on the gentle arch of her spine so that her straining body was clasped against his steely chest. She felt impatience rising within him; her struggles were only serving to accelerate his urge to accomplish what he had planned—her degradation, the assuaging of his lacerated pride.

'You must listen!' she gasped, with almost all the breath squeezed out of her. 'You've been drugged —Mattie showed me the love potion given to her by the obeah man. I told her to get rid of it, but something Camilla said upset her so much I feel sure she must have put it in your drink!'

Jacques held her away, sweeping her distraught face with a look of incredulity. 'Do you imagine I would allow any of the islanders' foul-smelling potions past my lips?' he scoffed, his contempt of her simplicity more convincing than his words.

She went very still. His conduct had been forgivable only because she had thought it unpremeditated, but if his disclaimer were true then his intention was to treat her like a wench—a bundle of anonymous femininity such as any sailor might pick up from any wharfside! Coldness such as she had never known snaked through her veins as for the first time she began to doubt whether she really knew the man whose reputed wickedness she had always been quick to deny. Ten years was a long time—long enough to scar the mind and embitter the soul of the boy she had loved. Even now, she was reluctant to relinquish her belief that the gossips had lied, that beneath the arrogant exterior beat a heart that ached for love and understanding, and for the comfort to be found in a woman's loving arms. But the satirical eyes confused her, the mouth framed with bitterness seemed incapable of appreciating lips that were gentle, and his grasp, roughly constricting, held no promise of tenderness but rather threatened to overpower ruthlessly any punitive attempt to resist. No woman would ever be accepted by him as an equal—a tyrant—he would be content with nothing less than an abject slave!

'Well?' He sounded as if he enjoyed the sport of baiting. 'Now that you have had time to examine my motives, what conclusion have you drawn?'

'I ...' When his head swooped to catch her words she strove to speak above a whisper. 'I think you meant to frighten me, and you've succeeded. But I wish you would believe me when I tell you that there's never been anything other than friendship between myself and Jeremy. I realize that what you

155

saw this evening could very easily have been mis-
construed and your anger is understandable. But
please,' her voice broke under the strain of being
dissected by piercing eyes, 'don't do anything you
might deeply regret.'

'To regret deeply is to live afresh!' he countered,
savage of being soothed.

Something snapped inside her, the tight band of
fear, perhaps, the tensity of overstrung emotions,
the long-tested endurance—whichever it was, the
break brought relief in a flood of reckless words.

'Why hanker for a fresh life when you've made
such a mess of the one you already have? You're
like a spoiled child, determined to kick out at
everything that displeases you because, although
you have all the material possessions you could possibly want, you've discovered money can't buy
happiness! I'm sorry for you,' she scathed. 'Poor,
rich playboy who's not having any fun! Earlier
this evening Camilla warned me to be ready to
abdicate in her favour. Well, she's welcome to you
—as far as I'm concerned our marriage can't end
soon enough!' She would have carried on, had not
a hard mouth clamped down upon hers, imposing
both silence and punishment. Jacques prolonged
the kiss to its bitter end, one hand gripping her
waist, the other stroking the velvet column of her
neck, stretched to the limit in her effort to evade
his touch.

'Sacré cœur!' Truly she had aroused the devil!
'First you must give our marriage time to begin!'

His dark head descended, intent upon plunder,
and as if at a signal the elements broke loose of

restraint. Gusting wind tore through the open window, lifting heavy curtains like strips of ribbon, sending a vase of crystal crashing to the floor in a frenzy of wild flapping. Thunder prowled like the grumbling of an enraged tiger around the Grand House perched upon a mountainside, illuminated by sudden flashes of lightning which to the girl inside were far less startling than the flame of the man driven by pride into claiming his rights as a husband.

Her frightened young eyes transmitted a plea for kindness as his lithe body levered her down, imprisoning her in the depths of a ruffled silken spread. But there was no softening in dark-lashed eyes, black as temper, cold as gems. She did not fight him—men are not born wolves, they become wolves, and his aggression was the result of deep mistrust, a conviction that women as individuals fell into either of two categories—witch or bitch!

Elise shuttered the tight, hot shell of her heart against his passionate words—endearments inspired in the spurious heat of love-madness and meant only to be written on running water or etched in sand. Desire gathered strength with the storm, a mingling of fear and ecstasy. The heavens wept as she wept, hail as cold as her heart rained down upon the house built by pirates and inherited by a man owning enough ruthless audacity to be dubbed a worthy heir.

Later she lay dry-eyed but inwardly weeping as the noise of the storm abated and was replaced by the sound of her husband's deep, steady breathing. He slept with his head cradled against her breast, one arm outflung as if aware. even in sleep, of the need of force to keep her there. As the storm had faded so had the holocaust of emotion that had flared hungrily as a fiery torch, devouring them both in flame. But the aftermath lacked contentment. No sense of peace soothed emotions still violently astir. Elise choked back a sob and closed her eyes, tears escaping closed lids, drowning a quivering mouth which, when she finally slept, retained its tremulous lines of unfathomable pain.

one arm outlining as if aware, even in sleep, of the
need of force to keep her there. As the storm had
faded so had the holocaust of emotion that

CHAPTER THIRTEEN

NEXT morning Elise awoke to find she was alone,
with only the indentation of a head on the adjoining pillow to provide evidence that the events of the
previous night were not just an agonizing night-
mare.

She forced herself to shower and picked at ran-
dom a dress of green cotton from the wardrobe
bulging with outfits, many still unworn. Shuddering
with distaste at the necessity of having to make use
of clothes heaped upon her as part-fulfilment of a
bargain, she slid shut the door and dressed quickly,
not bothering even to check her appearance before
hurrying downstairs.

It was nine o'clock and as Jacques was an early
riser, seldom to be seen around the house once the
sun lifted above the horizon, she felt no qualms
about making for the salon where she usually enjoyed a solitary breakfast. All she wanted was coffee,
hot, black and sweet, to steady racing pulses and
overwrought nerves, so she made straight for the
coffee pot, ignoring an array of dishes set out upon
a side table. Keeping her back to windows shuttered
against the glare of the sun, she sat down at the
table and raised the cup to her lips, only to have it
startled from her fingers by a grave observation
directed from somewhere behind her head.

'Shouldn't you at least try to eat a piece of toast?'

Too shocked to move, she remained staring at

the coffee stain spreading in an ever-widening circle around the shattered cup.

Muttering a small imprecation, Jacques strode forward and almost lifted her from her chair before grabbing a napkin to dam the flow of scalding liquid. Are you all right?' Thoroughly he examined her hands for blisters, then, satisfied that she was unmarked, he retained her hand in his clasp and continued his examination further, encompassing ashen cheeks, mouth red as a bruise, and large eyes darkened to black by haunting hurt.

A silence that was impenetrable fell between them; the effort of words was beyond her even though some mysterious instinct told her she had nothing physical to fear from the man whose fingers did not slacken from around his captive. Mutely she waited, wanting to hate him yet moved to compassion by evidence of suffering etched deeply into his stern features. If only he had heeded her warning, she thought dully, he would not now be experiencing bitter regret brought about by the knowledge that one night of revenge had cost him a lengthier separation from the girl he loved. Strangely, she had to fight an impulse to stroke away the lines scored around his eyes and mouth and to drive the desperation from his eyes with an assurance that whatever she could do to release him from his trap he had but to ask.

A thrill like wild, sweet music trembled through her veins as unwillingly she recalled one tender moment of daring when she had run her fingers through his crisp dark hair. And other fleeting memories that stung a rush of colour to her cheeks; cheeks that modesty had reddened.

'The colour of virtue . . .' He spoke gently as with a light finger he traced the progress of her blush.

She jerked away, tormented by the clamouring pride of a humiliated woman whose love had been dragged in the dust.

He flinched from the action, a flicker of pain disturbing his mouth which was quickly restored to its grim lines. 'I'm sorry,' he sounded shockingly strained. Then, concerned by her pallor, he offered, 'Let me get you some more coffee.'

But her limitations had been reached. Backing towards the door, she stammered a refusal. 'No, I don't want anything! Please excuse me, I'm going for a swim . . . !' Without waiting for permission, she sped out and across the hall as if a posse of devils were at her heels.

Not until she had reached the beach did she realize she had neither costume nor towel. Panting with exertion, she swung round to face in the direction from which she had come, and the sight of the Grand House, an admonishing finger raised in the distance, deterred her from making the return journey. She threw herself upon the beach and gazed longingly at the froth of water slaking the thirst of hot silver sand. She yearned to feel its healing caress, ached to immerse her body in its cooling swell. There had been a time when lack of costume would not have deterred her, but a strange new shyness cast an inhibiting shadow—even with the breadth of the beach between them, she felt Jacques' presence intimidatingly near.

161

Resigned to defeat, she lay back on the sand, but desire grew with the heat of the sun until finally a hazy mirage popped into her mind, a picture of her own room in her grandmother's cottage and inside a chest of drawers containing half a dozen rather disreputable swimsuits!

It was a long trek on foot and in the heat of day, but Elise was glad of a purpose with which to fill the empty hours. She took her time, walking as often as possible in the shade of trees, searching for fruit to ease the pangs of hunger, and drinking thirstily from occasional fresh-water streams. Only one human being passed her way, an island woman jogging along on the back of a mule transporting panniers of fresh water from a well to her home in a nearby village. Her wide grin and cheerful greeting were infectious, and Elise felt heartened enough to return the woman's greeting with a wave.

The cottage had a look of neglect, windows shuttered, doors firmly bolted, and in the deserted garden weeds ran riot through flowerbeds and beneath unpruned trees. Blinking away a tear, she pushed open the gate and trod the overgrown path leading to the back of the cottage. If nothing had been touched since her departure, she ought to be able to gain access through a scullery window whose faulty catch and rickety shutter had been the source of some annoyance to her grandmother.

She sighed her satisfaction when she rounded a corner and saw the shutter swinging open, hanging by one broken hinge. It took her barely a minute to clamber on to the sill and manipulate the catch so as to gain entry, and when eventually she stood inside, surrounded by familiar objects, the longing for her grandmother's loving counsel became so intense she dropped into a chair and loosened a storm of heartbroken tears upon the scrubbed-top kitchen table.

An hour passed before she felt any inclination to move. Hunger pangs were not helping to restore her spirits, so feeling far from optimistic she began rummaging through the cupboards, knowing Mattie had been ordered to clear them of every perishable item before they left. She felt triumph far in excess of her achievement when her groping fingers fastened upon a tin which after further investigation proved to contain soup, and felt rewarded beyond belief when a biscuit tin yielded crackers in an unopened airtight packet.

'Such a feast!' she congratulated herself. 'Bless dear old Mattie and her slaphappy ways!'

Once the soup and crackers had been demolished, she made her way to the small sitting-room where she and her grandmother had habitually retired after meals with their coffee. There was no coffee nor even a grain of tea, but water still ran from the taps, so she filled a tumbler to the brim and carried it to the windowseat, where after flinging wide the shutters she perched on her favourite seat overlooking the ocean.

Inevitably, whenever her mind was unoccupied, her thoughts winged to Jacques. With the water-cooled tumbler pressed against hot cheeks, she forced herself to relive the trauma of the previous night, her mind wincing from too deep an examination of moments inexpressibly dear. He had begun

163

with cudgel in hand, determine. to punish, but his roughness had been so fleeting as to be barely remembered. Most men love to pluck the blossoms from a flower but few, she knew instinctively, would have shown so much concern or exercised the same control to ensure that the bud would survive unbruised ...

Suddenly further thought was unbearable. She jumped from her seat and ran upstairs, then feverishly she stripped off her clothes, dragged a costume from the drawer and drew it over her shivering limbs before racing downstairs towards the beckoning, crescent-shaped cove.

The water was divine, buoyant and deliciously cool. For an hour Elise threshed about in its depths, revelling in the pleasure she had been frustrated from enjoying hours earlier. *Many* hours earlier, she reflected, noting with surprise the red ball of sun nearing the lip of the ocean. On impulse she began swimming out towards it, measured strokes giving her maximum propulsion through the water. It was a game to be enjoyed, a race to see how much distance she could cover before the red disc began slipping under the waves.

She was far from shore when cramp immobilized her legs. An agonized scream tore from her lips as she went under, then a second panic-stricken cry when she surfaced momentarily to suck in air. When she was dragged under for a third time she knew she was going to die and intense pain shot to her heart at the thought of not being given the chance to say a last goodbye. As she fought to the surface for one last glimpse of the island she loved, a name tore from her lips, sending a signal, a prayer, a plea for help echoing across the ocean.

She stirred and felt support beneath her clutching fingers. She held on to the lifeline, pulling herself free of clinging softness, and was surprised when the moan that escaped parted lips was not followed by an onrush of choking water.

'Relax, sweetie, you're quite safe!'

Her eyes flew open to search for the owner of the reassuring statement, and immediately her attention was riveted upon the ceiling above her head, the blankets around her body, the surrounding solidity of a bed.

'Where am I?'

'The classic opening remark of the semi-conscious!' came the cheerful rejoinder from the shadow hovering above her head. Jolted into awareness, she peered upward, then said flatly, 'Oh ... it's you.'

'Yes, it's I.' Jeremy's voice was dry. He reached out to check her pulse and she shrank back against her pillows, her eyes wary and not a little accusing. 'Don't worry,' he calmed. 'At a guess, I'd say my attentions have caused you enough trouble—and besides,' he informed her wryly, 'you're my patient, so any move from me could be regarded as highly unethical.' The sudden relaxation of her guard was unflattering. 'How are you feeling?' he questioned, hiding his hurt behind professional concern.

'Fine!' she sounded surprised. 'But how did I get here? The last thing I remember is water closing over my head.'

'Since I was summoned here urgently by the

rather savage Comte, I've managed to gather that for some reason he was out in his speedboat patrolling the coast when he spotted you struggling in the water. Why, and for what he was searching, I haven't yet discovered—likewise, the reason for your presence here alone at the cottage. 'Dare I hazard a guess,' he probed, 'that all is not well between you and the Comte and that, predictably, my behaviour last evening is the cause?' Goaded by the apprehension darkening her eyes, he stressed urgently, 'I meant every word I said last night, Elise, if there's the remotest chance for me please say . . .'

Lengthening silence told him she was searching for words to soften a blow. When she whispered, 'I'm sorry, Jeremy . . .' he winced, then shrugged as if shouldering a burden.

'Don't distress yourself, my dear,' he recovered far enough to make his reply light. 'Camilla satisfied me once, perhaps in time she may do so again. Strange,' he pondered, 'how well our scheme worked —except for the backlash, that is. Now that I'm no longer eager, Camilla is making all the running, and the same might be said to apply—' He broke off abruptly, unsure of his facts.

But ignoring his unfinished sentence, Elise jerked upright and contradicted fiercely, 'You must be mistaken—Camilla can't be interested in you, she's in love with Jacques and he with her!'

Jeremy shrugged. 'Then why has he been avoiding her these past weeks? Only last night while on our way to your home, she confessed that pressure of business had been keeping them apart.'

The business of playing watchdog to his wilful wife, Elise could have told him bitterly, a chore he had considered both necessary and frustrating. She did not communicate these thoughts to Jeremy, however; the effort of making conversation had sapped her energy and her eyelids felt so weighted she was finding it difficult to stay awake. 'I'm so tired,' she nestled into her pillow, stifling a yawn.

'Of course you are,' he agreed crisply. 'And now that I've ascertained that no permanent damage has been done I'll leave you to sleep and issue instructions that you're not to be disturbed by *anyone*. Not even your husband, who is even now pacing the passage outside of your door.'

'He is . . . !' Lashes flew up over eyes shocked wide open.

'And has been since I arrived,' Jeremy supplied, looking as if he intended guarding her from intrusion even at the risk of having to cross swords. 'A man as anxious as he must have guilt scored into his soul—it will do him no harm to suffer a little longer.'

'Guilt? Why should he suffer guilt on my account?' Elise flushed, wondering how much Jeremy actually knew.

'Because he drove you to it, I suppose,' he replied savagely, his damped-down anger finally overriding his patient's need to remain undisturbed.

But even though incensed and deeply suspicious, he could not fail to recognize genuine bewilderment when she questioned, 'Drove me to what? I've no idea what you're implying, but I can assure you Jacques was in no way to blame for my predicament. How could he be, no one can be expected to foresee or prevent the onset of cramp?'

'Cramp?' Jeremy was sceptical. 'Are you certain that's all it was, or are you, in your usual forgiving way, attempting to cover up the fact that his diabolical treatment drove you into attempting an irrevocable method of escape?'

Her horrified look caused him to falter, uncertainty cooling his rush of heated words. 'Don't look at me like that,' he muttered. 'I'm not alone in my suspicions. Jacques—who when I arrived seemed on the verge of insanity—let slip a remark which betrayed his belief that you had deliberately set out to take your own life.'

'Poor Jacques!' Her involuntary cry sounded the death knell of his hopes. For a startled second Jeremy searched her wan face, learning from a mouth quivering with pain being felt on behalf of another man that the hope he had cherished was futile. As he watched, two large tears forced their way from under her lashes and he backed away, cursing the twist of fate that had endowed such depth of affection upon an uncaring husband.

The rancour he felt was present in his voice when he confronted the man whose ceaseless prowling turned to immobility immediately he stepped into the passageway.

'She's going to be all right,' he informed the black-browed statue towering in the shadows. 'Go in to her if you must, but only for a moment—she needs sleep and most important a period of complete relaxation to counteract shock. I must beg you to be extra gentle with her, *monsieur*, provided it's in your nature to be so.' Jeremy awaited the response.

To his surprise the sneer was allowed to pass without comment; a glance of chilling dislike was all the response Jacques spared him before striding into the bedroom.

A sixth sense bestowed as extra protection upon the defenceless warned Elise that danger threatened. Beneath cool sheets her slim body became rigid even before a fan of lashes lifted from tear-wet cheeks. She looked up and was pinioned by eyes brooding darkly, making her instantly fretful of her weakness. She tried to project understanding in her glance, but failed to pierce the armour of aloofness protecting the man who thought himself twice crucified by the stigma of suicide. She struggled upright. A cool hand branded her shoulder as he pressed her back into the nest of pillows.

'Don't disturb yourself,' Jacques clipped the austere command. 'Sherlock insists that my visit must last no longer than a minute, but that will be sufficient time for me to say what is on my mind.' As if unable to bear the sight of her ashen face, he turned away and walked to the window, then, his back tense and unbending, he threw across his shoulder:

'I agree that the time has come for us to part. None of the unsavoury details of the divorce need concern you—I will instruct my solicitor to begin proceedings and I will supply all the evidence needed to get the case speeded as quickly as possible through court. Naturally, we can no longer reside under the same roof, so I suggest you remain here in the cottage which you can now regard as your home—I will see that the deeds are made over to you immediately. Naturally, I shall allow you sufficient funds to enable you to maintain a comfortable standard of living.'

Elise struggled to keep her expression blank as he strode towards her, determined that he would never know how mortally she was hurt by his decision to sever the bonds he found so restricting. She deserved his contempt; she had deceived him and from that first deceit had been born many others. Their marriage—a house built on air—had been fated to come tumbling to the ground.

'Very well,' she quavered on a deeply indrawn breath. 'I'll abide by whatever decision you make.'

Jacques' acknowledgement was sombre, not in the least reminiscent of a captive being freed of his chains.

As he walked to the door he halted to deliver one last bitter thrust. 'You'll be needing Mattie, I'll send her to you straight away. Doubtless, as well as being required as a nurse, she will be needed to play the role of chaperone!'

home—I will see that the debts are made over to
you immediately. Naturally I shall allow you sufficient funds to enable you to maintain a comfortable

CHAPTER FOURTEEN

THREE weeks later Jeremy paid Elise a visit. He
had attended regularly in his capacity as physician
during the week following her mishap, but gradually when it had become obvious that his patient's
hurt went far beyond the healing capacity of medi-
cine, his visits had become shorter and less fre-
quent.

He found her in the garden, stretched out on a
lounger placed beneath the shade of a flowering
ebony tree, its branches laden with a glorious pro-
fusion of yellow blossoms. Drugged by the scent
and by the peace of her surroundings, Elise lifted
one lazy eyelid at the sound of approaching footsteps, then with reluctance dragged herself erect
to offer a polite greeting.

'Good afternoon, Jeremy, how nice of you to call.'
He ignored her greeting—a falsely bright smoke-
screen thrown up to distract attention from wan
features and heavy eyes. She braved his inquisitive
look, but quivered when after looking his fill he
accused:

'Up until today, I had considered ladies pining
for lost loves to be figments of the imagination of
Victorian novelists.'

Elise flushed angrily. 'You ought to have been
one yourself, your fancies seem evocative of that
era!' He smiled, pleased by her show of spirit, but
the ease with which she had been manipulated

made her even angrier. 'Either sit down or go away!' she snapped when Jeremy continued grinning, looking, she thought, like a man whose brittle amusement might be covering a scar.

He dropped down beside her and proved her suspicions correct by directing what was almost accusation into his words. 'I've come to say goodbye. Tomorrow I'm leaving the island for good!'

She could not project regret because she felt none —nor relief either. Her emotions, thoroughly ravaged, had become so numbed that life was now being lived in a vacuum of day-to-day monotony, a cocoon within which she felt able to exist without having to endure the pain of actual living. She was jealous of her immunity, and had no intention of allowing Jeremy's unhappiness to threaten her peace of mind. 'Really? Then I hope you have a pleasant flight.'

'Stony-hearted witch!' he returned pleasantly, resigned to the fact that whoever might possess enough fire to melt her small frosted heart it was not he.

She relented. 'I'm sorry, Jeremy, that was unkind. I shall miss you very much—your kindness, your company ...'

'I wish you meant that!' He leant forward to take her hand. 'If I thought my presence here would help in any way I would stay—and ask nothing.'

Delicately, she disengaged his clasp. 'What was Camilla's reaction to your news?'

He shrugged. 'I haven't told her yet, I wanted you to be the first to know.' He bit back an explanation; obviously she was too uninterested to care that he had gambled on his decision stirring her into a a surprised protest—even into the discovery of an emotion far stronger than dismay. Her indifference dealt a bitter blow to his hope of taking her with him when he left.

'You've seen her recently?' He was astute enough to recognize the motive behind the casual question; an oblique way of asking if Camilla and Jacques were still meeting. He gained no satisfaction from replying, 'We've met occasionally for lunch, but her evenings are reserved solely for Jacques.'

Remorse stabbed him when Elise whitened. But it was better that she should face reality, painful though it was, than continue mourning the loss of a man who thought so little of his wife that he could shrug off her memory to the extent of making Kingston ring with tales of his amorous exploits. According to rumour, Camilla was but one of the string of females chosen for their sophistication and outstanding beauty to partner a man chasing after pleasure as if he feared its source might suddenly run dry. Night after night, he threw himself into a boisterous round of gaiety that seldom waned before dawn—but the punishing pace was beginning to tell in features thin-drawn and devoid of tan, in deeply sunken eyes and a mouth scored with lines of dissipation.

As he debated whether or not to acquaint her with the history of Jacques' debauchery, he was sidetracked by her observation:

'I can't really believe you when you say you no longer want Camilla. To deny love is not easy,' her voice lowered to a whisper. 'I know, I've tried . . . You've no idea how hard I've tried.'

This was not the moment to defend his case, she was too upset to listen to protestations that loving Camilla from afar had become a habit which, once having moved to closer quarters, had quickly died, starved by her inconsideration, by her selfishness and by the cool aloofness which had once attracted but now repelled. Instead, with the object of rescuing her from depression, he adopted a cheerful note.

'I really came to ask if you'll join me this evening in a farewell dinner. Please don't say no,' he pleaded, reading refusal in her frown, 'I can't stand the idea of spending my last evening dining alone, probably finishing off with a solitary meander around town. I'm lonely, Elise, and not a little down, please take pity and say you'll come!'

Her strongest impulse was to refuse. Sympathy she could spare, but he had no right to expect her to relinquish the safety of her cocoon to venture into places where she might be confronted by the man who never failed to leave her bruised. Appalled by the very thought, she shook her head to deny the favour, but the cloud that descended upon his face made her weaken. During the past weeks his many acts of kindness had rekindled the trust and affection she had earlier felt. Tomorrow he would be gone for good, to commit him to a last solitary evening would be a churlish thing to do.

'Very well,' he would never know what it cost her to agree, 'on condition that we dine somewhere quiet away from the crowds . . .'

'I know the very place!' he assured her eagerly.

'I'll pick you up at eight.' At that, he departed.

Many times during the afternoon she was tempted to send a message retracting her acceptance, but an innate sense of fair play would not allow her to spoil the transient happiness of his few remaining hours. Mattie had been vociferous in her approval, and her features were wreathed in smiles when she entered the sitting-room to remind Elise, 'Seven o'clock gone, honey, time to get dressed!'

She stirred, irritated by Mattie's enthusiasm and by her own reluctance to be pried from the safety of her shell. 'There's plenty of time, I'm not going to a ball, just a simple dinner for two.'

'Greedy choke puppy!' Mattie chuckled, enormously pleased that her charge was being coaxed out to eat. Not with even the most succulent of dishes had she been able to tempt her appetite over the past weeks, and the resultant slenderness of her charge was causing great anxiety to the old Jamaican whose criterion of health was ample curves and plump cheeks.

Momentarily a smile flickered across Elise's face, then died, leaving it even more pinched than before. 'Enough is as good as a feast' could apply to more than food, and her body grew cold at the reminder that tonight she was being forced to venture into Kingston, the pirates' lair favoured by the man whose presence alone was enough to tighten bands of fear around her throat . . .

She chose a dress to suit her mood, black chiffon over a stiff, rustling underskirt, the stark, unadorned material narrowing her willowy limbs to

175

the substance of a shadow. Against the pallor of her cheeks her mouth contrasted carnation-pink, a crushed flower trembling in a breeze of distress that feathered her warm skin with the whispered warning: *Don't go!* Every instinct urged her to obey, but she was committed. When the doorbell echoed its summons through the house she grabbed a wrap and ran downstairs to meet Jeremy, determined that tonight she would be as gay and brilliant as the butterflies embroidered on the shawl draped across her shoulders.

The restaurant he had chosen was tucked away in a quiet side street. When they entered the proprietor escorted them into the discreetly luxurious interior, Oriental in ambience, with flocked wallcoverings of dark wine interlaced with gold, hanging Chinese lanterns that cast a circle of soft light on to each individual table and weird background music pitched low so as not to intrude upon conversation, yet audible enough to fill any of the awkward silences that are apt to occur.

'I hope you like Chinese food?' Jeremy looked anxious as he helped her off with her wrap.

'I adore it.' She relieved both him and the proprietor who was handing her the menu. After much deliberation and some outrageous leg-pulling by Jeremy they ordered Go Lo Yuk, a name Elise swore he had invented for her amusement but which turned out to be a dish of sweet-sour pork so delicious that amusement took second place to the serious business of eating. Laughter had made her hungry, and she found to her surprise that she could manage the portion of figs and cream Jeremy insisted upon ordering. It was not until coffee had been poured into minute dragon-painted cups that he became serious, his taut jawline outlined by the flame touched to the cigar clenched between his teeth.

'In many ways, I'll be sorry to leave,' he brooded, flickering the charred match into an ashtray. 'When I first came to the island three years ago, I told myself I'd found the nearest thing to heaven. Nothing on earth would ever make me return to the rat race, I decided, and for the rest of my life I would live my days in earthly paradise and be perfectly contented with my lot.'

'Why did you change your mind?' she queried softly, sensing his need to reminisce.

'You helped, my dear,' he startled her by saying. 'The only known antidote to unrequited love is work, work and more work, and that is the reason I've decided to return to England where I'll find all the facilities necessary for the advancement of my career. I intend to specialize, and that will mean working all day and studying at night, with hardly a moment to spare for thoughts of what might have been.'

'I'm sorry, Jeremy ...'

'No need to be.' He reached out to stroke away the pucker creasing her brow. 'To be quite honest, even before I met you doubts had begun to form. My feelings for you merely accelerated the need I felt for more positive action. Nothing palls so quickly as pleasure—my work here was too undemanding, I was beginning to feel ashamed of allowing my capabilities to rot. Think of me in a few years from now,' he twinkled, reverting to his former gaiety, 'with my name etched on a brass plate in Harley Street, a chauffeur-driven Rolls and perhaps even a knighthood bestowed for my contributions to society. Sir Jeremy Sherlock! Sounds good, eh?'

'You are a fool!' she chuckled, 'but such a dear, clever fool.' Earnestness replaced laughter. 'I believe in you, Jeremy, I know you'll achieve all you set out to do—yes, even the knighthood! Some day, I'll shatter the calm of the ladies' tea circle by casually dropping your name into the conversation: *My old friend, Sir Jeremy Sherlock, you know ...!'*

They were still laughing when they left the restaurant to walk to the car. Fear had completely left her, and as he nosed out into the traffic, heading for home, she relaxed in her seat, still smiling. Time passed quickly on the return journey as they engaged in the companionable conversation of friends completely at ease with one another and lapsed into comfortable silences full of pleasant thought. Bright moonlight was flooding the cottage and garden as they drew up before the front gate, every bush and shrub clearly outlined. No light shone through the windows, so guessing Mattie must have retired early, Elise did not demur when he murmured, 'Stay awhile, let's prolong this most enjoyable evening.'

'It has been fun, hasn't it?' she agreed. 'Thank you so much for asking me.'

'Persuading you, don't you mean?' he contradicted, sliding an arm across the back of her seat.

'Don't spoil it ...!' she begged when his lips hovered a mere kiss away.

He grimaced, his eyes upon her troubled face. 'What will you be doing when I'm gone?' he urged. 'When I think of you—which will be often—how shall I picture you? What plans have you made for the future?'

'None, as yet ...' She swallowed hard. 'I intend living each day as it comes.'

'Sweetheart!' he groaned, settling his arm around her shoulders, 'I'm worried about you! Please come with me, I swear all I want is to look after you!'

'This is my home,' she returned simply. 'I'd rather die than leave here.'

A long silence spelt out his acceptance of her answer. Then desperately, when she stirred, he begged, 'May I kiss you goodbye—just one kiss to cherish and remember ...?'

She hesitated fractionally, then lifted her face to his, experiencing a rush of warm feeling when his lips touched hers in a passionless, reverent caress. 'Goodbye!' she whispered, close to tears, before jumping out of the car and running quickly into the house.

Once inside, she stood with her back pressed against the wall of the darkened hall listening to the revving of the engine, the swishing of tyres, then finally the noise of the car fast receding into the distance. If her heart had not already been dead a bit of it would have broken there and then. Listlessly, she moved towards the stairs, hoping sleep might ease her throbbing head, but just as her foot descended upon the first stair she stiffened, staring wide-eyed at a figure that had detached itself from the shadows and begun walking towards her.

'Jacques!' she gasped, her hand flying to restrain the pulse jumping madly in her throat. 'How long have you been here?'

When he moved closer his frame took on the substance of granite, his face cold and grey, with eyes of matching slate. 'Long enough to witness the touching farewell,' he grated, holding on to his composure with great effort.

She brushed past him, a wraith in the darkness, resentment of his arbitrary manner written in every line of her proudly tilted head and slim, unyielding body. Sweeping into the salon, she switched on a lamp, then nodded, indicating a chair.

'You may sit down, if you wish. I know that whatever business brings you here it will not take long to explain, so I won't offer you a drink.'

Jacques was almost as nonplussed as she had intended, but not quite—the Comte de Montague was not one to be intimidated by a woman, however freezing her manner. He was sufficiently wise, however, to decide upon a change of tactics, so keeping a keen eye on his haughty, infinitely more mature wife, he opted for a less arrogant approach.

She was taken aback by his strained, almost diffident tone of voice. 'Before you leave the island,' he missed her start of surprise, 'there is something I want to explain.'

'Oh, yes?' From the safety of her shell she chanced a look, and was appalled at the sight of his haggard features, embittered mouth and eyes, piercing as ever, but reflecting an emotion so intense they seemed to burn with blue flame. Not even the coolness, the almost impudent negligence of her

reply, aroused him to anger. He regarded her steadily, seeing resentment where once he had seen love,
rebellion on lips which previously had pleaded
for his kisses and the slender body he had possessed
arched as if to shy away from his touch. Flushing
darkly, he looked away.

'The girl in Paris,' he began, rendering her dumb
with surprise, 'we were students together. I never
knew her really well, she was one of a crowd yet
always one apart. For some reason, she aroused my
pity and also, being very much an inexperienced
newcomer, I was grateful for her company at func-
tions which otherwise I would have had to attend
alone.'

Staring straight ahead, he admitted simply, 'I was
warned by those who knew her well not to become
too involved—it seems she had a history of unbal-
anced behaviour and an unhappy love affair the
previous term had affected her deeply. I shrugged
off the advice, knowing she and I were never fated
to share more than lukewarm friendship, and for
months we continued in this vein, asking and receiv-
ing nothing of each other except companionship
and the satisfaction of shared interests. Never once
during that time did I suspect her unhappiness
was suicidal—no one was more shocked than I when
her body was pulled out of the Seine ...'

'How dreadful ...!' Her cry of distress was involuntary.

He stirred, disturbed out of his reverie, and
Elise stumbled out the question, 'But why were you
blamed—a mere acquaintance who took pity on a
lonely girl!'

'She left a note—a scribbled, distracted note—telling of her misery, her shame, and her sense of desertion. All she omitted was the name of her lover, so as we had been seen so much together people naturally assumed . . .

'But your friends, the other students, they must have known!'

'They were never amongst my accusers—indeed, they protested my innocence loud and long, but the scandalmongers refused to listen. Even after the inquest, when the true facts had been established, there were those who insisted that my grandfather had used his influence to shield my guilt. Gossip has wings,' he assured her bitterly, 'my reputation today is built upon the surmise that every scandalous tale is built on firm foundations.'

'How unfair!' she clenched, stamping down an urge to comfort the tensely held figure. 'But why are you telling me this? You must know I never doubted your innocence.'

His glance swung in her direction, stabbing as a rapier. 'Never?' he scoffed. 'Not even when my cruelty drove you into attempting to take your own life? I was demented that day,' the words rasped painfully from his throat. 'I wanted to explain, but you rushed out of the house without giving me the chance, so I began looking for you——' He broke off, beads of sweat standing on his forehead as he relived the hours of searching and their final, agonizing conclusion.

'But I never had any intention of taking my own life!' she protested. 'I rushed out of the house that morning without waiting to pick up a swimsuit. I was lying on the beach longing for a swim when suddenly I recalled the spare suits I'd left here at the cottage, so I set off to walk,' she faltered, alarmed by his immobile attention to her every word. Sending him an anxious glance, she continued cautiously, 'Hours later I arrived at the cottage, hungry and thirsty. Foolishly, I had a meal immediately before going into the water and it must have been that, combined with fatigue, which was responsible for the cramp that seized my legs. So you see,' she stressed, 'the accident was due entirely to my own folly and would never have occurred had I been sensible enough to go back to the Grand House.'

'Where the man you hated was waiting ...!' he clamped. His ravaged face was playing havoc with her emotions, but Elise held back, safeguarding the barricade of ice around her heart. It almost cracked, however, when Jacques asked in a voice not quite steady, 'Is that the truth? Is that *honestly* how it happened ...?'

'I swear it.' She could barely force the words past the lump in her throat.

Relief lifted like a cloud from his face, and for a second she glimpsed the lighthearted boy whose passing she so much regretted. But when he reached out to touch her she shrank back and immediately his hand dropped to his side, a dark tide of colour rising beneath his skin.

'I deserved that,' he admitted, unclenching his fist to search his inner pocket for a case from which he selected a cheroot. She dared not look at him as he lit the tip and inhaled deeply, but she was vividly conscious of his projected hurt.

He stood up, and keeping the width of the room between them he began to speak, unemotionally, as if acquainting her of facts he felt she was entitled to know.

'I hurt you very much—yet I can offer no valid excuse. I used you to purge my disillusionment of all your sex. I felt the punishment was justified because of the scene I had interrupted earlier that night, and though I would have preferred to have vented my spleen on Sherlock he was not there, and my sense of betrayal was screaming out for immediate revenge.' Hardly daring to breathe, Elise strained to hear when his voice dropped on the incredible words, 'However, things did not turn out quite as I had planned—when I pulled you into my arms I fell into your hands ... such gentle, loving hands.' He paused to draw in a shuddering breath before releasing the admission. 'My punishment was to discover too late that I had tried to destroy the only creature I have ever deeply loved.'

Every instinct rebelled against her determination not to respond to the need and regret in Jacques' words. Once before she had been tricked into his arms by a strong play upon her sympathies—she could not bear the thought of facing the same humiliation again. Silence stretched intolerably long while doubts crowded her mind, throwing her senses into a whirl. Faintly, she heard him mention Jeremy's name, and she tensed, expecting anger.

'Don't worry, I have no intention of putting obstacles in the way of your happiness. I know Sherlock is leaving tomorrow, I shall not prevent you from joining him.'

The clamped promise was all the assurance she needed. Eyes of glowing amber fastened upon his grave face as wildly she berated, 'Thank you very much, but I don't happen to want Jeremy, I want you!'

As if at the crack of a whip, his head jerked upwards, his look *daring* her to torment. He remained so still she began to wonder for a hurtful, hysterical moment if she had misunderstood, if the long, agonizing silence was a prelude to yet another humiliating rebuff.

She did not see him move, only felt the exquisite agony of his grip upon her arms and heard the hoarse rasp of his voice as he pleaded—*actually pleaded!*—'Elise, *mon cœur, mon petit amour*, I deserve any punishment, but please do not prolong the agony! *Tell me*, were those words words of love —or words of revenge?'

'Oh, my darling . . .' she whispered brokenly, feeling the heat of his desire melting the last icicle around her vulnerable heart.

'Elise, *ma petite* . . .' Jacques seemed almost afraid to abandon his rigid control. Tenderly he kissed her with his eyes; her soft, tremulous mouth, her smooth flushed cheeks, her long, curling lashes. Then with violent, physical force the dam broke and she was borne against his heart by a flood of passion, buffeted, drowned by his kisses, made breathless by his forceful compelling demands. Finally he was convinced, and he rocked her trembling body in his arms, gently kissing away each tear of happiness from her cheeks. His groaned: 'Oh, my darling, I've *missed* you so!' was sweeter than any love song, more moving than a sonnet, more beautiful than anything she had ever heard.

She laughed, a breathless, husky laugh, and quickly his lips swooped to the hollow of her throat, seeking to capture the small sound. She clung to him, ecstatic with happiness, yet regretful of all the wasted hours. 'Why must love hurt so much, my darling?' she whispered, her lips against his only visible scar.

'Nothing can be mended that has not been torn apart, *ma petite ange*, but don't be afraid,' he kissed the frown from her brow, 'no future pain could possibly exceed that which we have so foolishly inflicted upon each other. We are healed of suffering because we have experienced it to the full.'

His head descended, intent upon blotting out painful memories, and as their lips clung his kiss said many things: it was at once a promise to adore, an oath of fidelity, a confession of capture and a deep and binding seal of commitment.

Later, as they prepared to leave for the Grand House, Jacques hugged his sleepy wife and cherished her with a smile. 'Many things remain unsaid, *mon ange*,' he whispered, 'but before we leave I wish to renew the promise I made many years ago, this time solemnly—not as a boy would to a girl, but as an adoring husband to his precious and most enchanting bride.'

Romance
is
Beautiful

Get to the
HEART OF
HARLEQUIN

HARLEQUIN READER SERVICE is your passport to The Heart of Harlequin . . .

if You...

 enjoy the mystery and adventure of romance then you should know that Harlequin is the World's leading publisher of Romantic Fiction novels.

 want to keep up to date on all of our new releases, eight brand new Romances and four Harlequin Presents, each month.

 are interested in valuable re-issues of best-selling back titles.

are intrigued by exciting, money-saving jumbo volumes.

 would like to enjoy North America's unique monthly Magazine "Harlequin" — available **ONLY** through Harlequin Reader Service.

are excited by **anything new** under the Harlequin sun.

then...

YOU should be on the Harlequin Reader Service — **INFORMATION PLEASE** list — it costs you nothing to receive our news bulletins and intriguing brochures. Please turn page for news of an **EXCITING FREE OFFER.**

a Special Offer for You...

just by requesting information on Harlequin Reader Service with absolutely no obligation, we will send you a "limited edition" copy, with a new, exciting and distinctive cover design — **VIOLET WINSPEAR'S** first Harlequin Best-Seller

LUCIFER'S ANGEL

You will be fascinated with this explosive story of the fast-moving, hard-living world of Hollywood in the 50's. It's an unforgettable tale of an innocent young girl who meets and marries a dynamic but ruthless movie producer. It's a gripping novel combining excitement, intrigue, mystery and romance.

A complimentary copy is waiting for YOU — just fill out the coupon on the next page and send it to us to-day.

Don't Miss...

any of the exciting details of The Harlequin
Reader Service—COLLECTOR'S YEAR...

♥ It promises to be one of the greatest publishing
   events in our history and we're certain you'll want
   to be a part of it.

♥ Learn all about this great new kind of series.

♥ Re-issues of some of the earliest, and best-selling
   Harlequin Romances.

♥ All presented with a new, exciting and distinctive
   cover design.

To become a part of the Harlequin Reader Service
INFORMATION PLEASE list, and to learn more about
COLLECTOR'S YEAR — simply fill in the coupon below
and you will also receive, with no obligation, Violet
Winspear's LUCIFER'S ANGEL.

SEND
TO:

Harlequin Reader Service,
"Information Please",
M.P.O. Box 707,
Niagara Falls, New York 14302.

CANADIAN
RESIDENTS

Harlequin Reader Service,
Stratford, Ont. N5A 6W4.

Name: _____

Address: _____

City: _____ State/Prov.: _____

Zip/Postal Code: _____

IP 206